Books by William Kingshart

The Changeling

The Dreaming Spires

I0548882

The Dreaming Spires

ISBN # 978-1-78686-301-0

©Copyright William Kingshart 2017

Cover Art by Posh Gosh ©Copyright 2017

Interior text design by Claire Siemaszkiewicz

Finch Books

Published in 2017 by Finch Books, Think Tank, Ruston Way, Lincoln, LN6 7FL, United Kingdom.

The Changeling

THE DREAMING SPIRES

WILLIAM KINGSHART

Dedication

This book is dedicated to my beautiful daughter Aisling.
My daughter — and daughter also to the moon.
With all my love, always.

Runs it not here, the track by Childsworth Farm,
Past the high wood, to where the elm-tree crowns
The hill behind whose ridge the sunset flames?
The signal-elm, that looks on Ilsley Downs,
The Vale, the three lone weirs, the youthful Thames?—
This winter-eve is warm,
Humid the air! leafless, yet soft as spring,
The tender purple spray on copse and briers!
And that sweet city with her dreaming spires,
She needs not June for beauty's heightening.

Thyrsis, Matthew Arnold

Chapter One

I looked upon my new school with apprehension. I, like everybody else, had seen Harry Potter, and I knew what went on under those gabled arches – in those shady, echoing, oak-paneled halls. For the past fourteen years, I had fought, played and studied – sometimes – in the wide, airy spaces of the American educational system. Now, at the age of seventeen, I had been transported here to something more ancient and terrible than I could ever have imagined – the Anglo-American School at Oxford, in England. It stood coolly aloof with its ivy-covered gray stone, its leaded windows and many tall chimneypots and ignored me.

I looked back at the Jeep I'd just climbed out of. Through the open passenger window, I could see Rosie, as English as tea and muffins. She was pretty, demure and drop-dead gorgeous. And, at twenty-five, disturbingly young to be my brand-new stepmother.

Terrifyingly, she winked at me and said, "Go knock 'em dead, Jake."

I watched the car disappear down the road, shouldered my bag then made my way through the great iron gates and down the short gravel drive between the perfect English lawns on either side. *Keep your head down*, I told myself, *and with any luck, nobody will notice you.*

But this was a school that specialized in diplomat's kids or the children of international businessmen and women, and their population was mainly transient. The norm for them was new faces that hung around for maybe a term or two then disappeared again. Mine was just another unremarkable face, passing through. I spent the morning in grateful anonymity, trying to get my bearings, and at one o'clock, I was wandering down a long, oak-paneled corridor, elbowing my way through talking, laughing, milling crowds, trying to find the canteen.

"Norgard, isn't it? The new chap."

The voice made me stop and turn. He was about my age, tall and well built with an easy smile. He was holding out his hand. I took it and we shook.

"Pendrake, Sebastian Pendrake."

"Hi, yeah, I'm Jake… Jake Norgard." I hesitated.

He said, "You look lost."

I smiled. "I guess I am. I'm looking for the canteen."

"You mean the Luncheon Hall. Come with me. We'll eat together and I'll tell you all about this place—whom to befriend and whom to avoid like the plague."

The Luncheon Hall was as vast as it was old. It had a high, gabled ceiling with ancient wooden beams. The walls were oak-paneled, like most of the school, and students sat at long oak benches and helped themselves to food from a buffet. You had the feeling that you wanted to call everything 'venerable'. Sebastian led me to the venerable buffet and handed me a venerable tray.

"Don't have the lamb. It's dreadful here. I'll take you to Glorfindel's in town if you're partial to lamb. Damned good. Have the beef. Cook's a dab hand with beef. Spuds are good, too, though his mash is lamentable. And you must have the sticky toffee pudding. It's traditional. You chaps haven't got it over there."

"Would you call it 'venerable'?"

He raised an eyebrow at me. "Venerable sticky toffee pudding? Indeed, I would."

We sat and he waved his fork around, looking in the general direction of the ceiling. "One of Oxford's newer buildings—only about five hundred years old but said to be on much older foundations. The original monastery that stood here may be Norman." He glanced at me like

8

he wasn't sure I knew what that meant then added, "That would make it—"

"I know who the Normans were, Sebastian. It would make it nearly a thousand years old."

He smiled. "Don't take offense, old chap. Even the English are forgetting their history." He sat back, dabbing his mouth with his paper napkin. "Nobody, for example, remembers that the Normans were not French—thank heavens—but Danish Vikings. And incidentally, you yourself must have Viking roots with a name like Norgard."

The beef was as good as he'd said, so I wasn't paying much attention to what he was rambling on about. I spoke absently, to my plate, "I do? I didn't know that—"

But before I'd finished, he was talking again. "Ah, that's the chap to avoid—him and his crony."

I looked up and followed his gaze. Two guys had just walked in. They were built like what Sebastian would probably call brick loos. The biggest was probably six foot six with shoulders like a gorilla. His neck was as wide as his head, and he had a hard jaw and real short white-blond hair. I couldn't see from where I was sitting, but two got you twenty he had very pale-blue eyes. His pal was just a smaller version of him.

Sebastian was saying, "Enter the Fourth Reich. That's Freddy 'Brutus' Muller. He's the captain of the American football team, and his nasty sidekick is Darren Barry Engels, otherwise known as DB."

I knew the type. I'd lived with them since I'd started school. Every school kid does, except the Brutuses of this world. They go on to become attorneys—and sometimes presidents. I shrugged. "If you ignore them, they usually ignore you."

He grunted. "I had a run-in with him once. He broke my nose"—his eyes glazed and he gave a funny smile—"but he sang soprano in the shower for a few weeks after that. Now we avoid each other."

I looked at Brutus. He was pushing to the head of the

line at the buffet. I said, "You mean you kicked him in his brains?"

He took a spoon to his sticky toffee pudding, still smiling. "You could say that."

The pudding was everything he had said it would be. And as I cleaned the bowl, I thought maybe I could grow to like Harry Potter land.

* * * *

The afternoon passed quickly, and before I knew it, I was shouldering my way through milling crowds toward the exit. That's when I saw her. You read about all that stuff that's supposed to happen—your heart skips a beat, time stands still, you know it's your destiny that you are soul mates, there will never be anyone else...yadda yadda yadda. And you laugh and mock and stick your fingers down your throat.

Wrong. When it happens, it happens just like that. It's all true.

I stood like a total chump and stared at her. She was the cutest thing I had ever seen. Everything about her was kind of wrong, but the way she put it together was perfection. She had red hair that was just auburn enough to look good. She had pale skin and freckles on an elfin face that made your belly burn like you'd been eating Carolina Reapers for breakfast. Her eyes were green and she had a cute little body that had exactly nothing wrong with it.

My heart skipped a beat. Time stood still. I knew.

She had stopped at the top of the stairs that led down to the drive and she seemed to be waiting. I was about to go over when I saw her smile at someone. I looked and my heart sank. Brutus and his sidekick DB swaggered over to her. I couldn't hear what he was saying, but by the leer on his face, it wasn't anything you'd say to your Great-aunt Hilda. I watched her face for her reaction and willed her to slap him, but she didn't. She laughed like she thought he was funny. He winked at her and I read, "Catch you around," on his lips as he strolled away. I felt sick.

I told myself girls just don't understand what jackasses guys can be, steeled myself and sauntered over to her with a big, friendly smile. "Hi, I'm Jake. I'm new here."

She kind of smiled then waited, like she wanted me to come to the point. I asked, "What's your name?"

"Ciara,"

I thought I caught a soft brogue and asked, "Is that an Irish accent?"

"It might be. Is yours American?"

"Yeah. I'm from San Francisco originally. How about you?"

Was it a twinkle in her eye or was it just contempt? She watched me for a beat with a shadow of a smile and said, "No, I'm not from San Francisco." Then she said, "There's my ride," and she was skipping down the steps.

I called after her, "I'll see you around…"

She glanced over her shoulder at me with that odd, indefinable look that could be either a brush of Irish lips or a kick in the nuts and said, "You might."

And she was gone.

A strong hand rested on my shoulder and Sebastian's voice brought me back from hell. "Now, that was unwise, old chap."

"Who cares?" I said with feeling.

"To be wise and love exceeds man's might."

"Who is she?"

"All you need to know about Ciara Fionn is that Brutus wants her, and if you stand in his way, he will do terrible things to you."

I saw Rosie's Jeep pull up outside the gate as Ciara climbed into a Jaguar across the road and drove away. I turned to face Sebastian, who was watching me with a smile that only the English know how to do. I said, "I know. But you know what?"

"I fear I do. You don't care, do you?"

I shook my head and told him, "I'll see you tomorrow, Sebastian. Hang loose."

We drove in silence for a while and I tried not to squirm. Having a gorgeous twenty-five-year-old stepmom when you're seventeen, even if you've just fallen helplessly in love for the rest of your life, is not easy, especially when she keeps looking at you with a cute smile on her face. That was what Rosie kept doing now.

She said, "So…?"

I glanced at her and had no idea what to say.

She added, "Did you meet any cute girls?" I swallowed and squirmed. "I bet they were queuing up for a handsome young devil like you, weren't they?"

I made a noise that started out full of good intentions to be a laugh, but ended up horribly strangled in my nose. When she heard it, she was compassionate enough to change the subject, and said, "You remember your father and I are having drinks with the dean this evening, so you'll be at home alone until about nine."

I struggled to master my vocal chords and said, in a voice that was ridiculously low and gravelly, "Yeah, sure…"

She pulled up outside our house. I fell out of the Jeep and bolted for the door.

I'm fairly sure they stopped building in Oxford somewhere about the sixteenth century. Certainly, anything they did build after that was not considered good enough for anyone with money, because anyone with money in Oxford lives in a house that is at least five hundred years old. And if you're super rich, it's even older than that. If Bill Gates was from Oxford, he'd live in a cave.

Our house was, I guess, pretty cool. Rosie told me it was late Tudor, which meant it was built around the time that Elizabeth I was beating up on the Spanish and stealing all the gold they'd stolen from the Incas. It had been renovated since then, but it was still all ancient oak beams, and part of the roof was still thatched. The door was original, five-hundred-year-old oak with massive iron-studded hinges, and the fireplace in the drawing room was so big you could stand in it.

The house was listed now, so you couldn't change it, but back in the thirties, someone had put French windows in the drawing room, so you could step out onto the landscaped garden. When I went in, the house was silent and very still. The French windows were open, so I stepped out onto the lawn to try to stop having inappropriate thoughts about Rosie and indulge in some very appropriate ones about Ciara. There was a stone-flagged path through the rose garden and I followed it, stopping to smell the buds and thinking of her curious smile and the soft sparkle in her eyes. At the end, it came to an arbor at the back of the garden, where a weeping willow bowed over the pond. Dusk was closing in, and a blackbird on the chimney was singing into the failing September light. I wished it was a nightingale or at least a lark. That's the kind of mood I was in. A blackbird's song is easily as beautiful as a nightingale's, but when you're in love for the first and last time in your life, it has to be a nightingale.

What you really don't want is an electromagnetic portal to a parallel universe to open over the garden bench in your arbor and a nine-foot Irish gnome to appear, chewing on a leg of lamb. You really don't want that to happen, but it happened to me on my first day in Oxford, the city of dreaming spires.

Chapter Two

It started as a pale, green glow that seemed to come from an invisible source and hovered over the garden bench. Then the air seemed to move weirdly. First, it was like it was wavering, then it started to swirl — slow to begin but then faster and faster into a spiral or vortex with its epicenter slipping down toward the seat of the bench. There was a violent crackling sound, wild sparks and a sudden, howling, whistling squall. The willow still bowed down into the pond and I thought I'd be blown off my feet. Then the air seemed to shatter, there was a loud explosion and there, sitting on the bench, chewing on a leg of lamb, was the weirdest thing I had ever seen in my life.

For want of a better word, I'd have to say he was a guy — a man — but he really *wasn't*. He was huge — and I really mean *huge*. When he eventually stood, I figured he was about nine feet tall. His body was a bit like the Hulk, if the Hulk stopped going to the gym. And he wasn't green. He was a kind of yellowish-brown. Each of his feet was about the size of two laptops. His hands were like ten-pound sacks of potatoes, and his head and face looked as though a giant condom had been stuffed with walnuts.

He tore off a hunk of meat with his teeth, chewed a moment and realized I was there, staring at him. He grinned through a mouth full of broken tombstones and torn meat. He wiped his mouth with the back of his arm and said what sounded like, "*Kay-ed meelah, fallcha row-it!*"

I said, "What the f...?" as my legs started to tremble uncontrollably and I sank slowly to the ground till I was sitting on the grass. A horrible noise issued from his throat, which I eventually realized was laughter.

"You don't remember me, do you, lad – or the old tongue? Got any ale there?"

I just gaped and a made strange, amputated noise.

He watched me a bit then spat on the grass. "Get a grip, lad. I'm Gorm. Remember?" He laughed again. "My own memory isn't all that good, I confess!" His face contorted and his left eye bulged at me as he leaned forward. "But *I* have an excuse. *I'm* three thousand years old" – he sat back and picked at his teeth with a long fingernail – "give or take a century. But you? You're naught but a wee whippersnapper!"

I said, "Am…am….am…"

"What?"

"Am I hallucinating? Am I having a psychotic break?"

He opened his mouth, screwed up his eyes and made a noise like a thousand bulls with cattle prods stuck where they really didn't want them. He was laughing again. "*Feck off* are ya! Feckin' psy-feckin'-chotic feckin' break! Ye feckin' gobshite! Only *humans* get psychotic coz of their brains, see? They're so feckin' narrow! Anything that isn't" – and he made a square box shape with his hands as he spoke – "in the wee-tidy box drives them *crazy!* They lose it, I tell yiz."

He set to chewing on his leg of lamb again. I watched him a moment and said, "I am. I'm crazy. I'm sitting here in the garden talking to a nine-foot gnome called Gorm about how people can't think outside the box."

He swallowed then belched loudly, causing the pond to ripple. "Gorm Chompsky, at your service. It was I who brought you to this world. I, who cared for you during your first days."

"Chompsky?" I began to laugh. "So you are Gnome Chompsky?"

"The very same!"

"Now I know I'm crazy." We sat in silence, one disturbed only by his chewing and belching, and slowly his words began to filter through to me. I said, "Wait…"

He cocked his head but continued chewing.

I said again, "Wait. Remember you? *Remember* you? How could I re… *Brought* me here? What do you mean *brought* me here?"

"Sure. Do you remember *nothing?* Jaysus!" He slapped his forehead with his palm and said something that sounded like, "*A vaw jean, tho-wur fy-adh dhum!* Do you not remember me bringing yiz here when you was no more than two years old?"

I stood and threw my arms in the air. "Of course I don't! A, I don't remember when I was two. And B, I wasn't *here* when I was two. I was in—"

He looked surprised. "You don't remember when you was two? Neither do I, as a matter of fact, but then *I'm* three thousand years old."

"Stop saying that. You are not— You *cannot* be three thousand years old. *Nobody* is three thousand years old."

He raised a horrible eyebrow at me and looked down at his vast, knobby body, then back at me.

"Okay," I said, "nobody *looks* like you, either. Nobody is a *gnome* like you. Nobody is…*can* be…like…*you!*" I flopped to the ground again and buried my face in my hands. "This isn't happening. This can't be happening. It isn't…"

There was silence for a bit and I began to think that maybe, when I opened my eyes, he'd be gone. A loud belch told me I was wrong. I looked up and all ghastly seven hundred and twenty-nine cubic feet of him was still there. He'd finished the meat and was gnawing on the bone. "Are you done? Only I have to get back. Did I ask if you had ale? My memory ain't what it was."

I despaired, and with despair came a strange kind of peace. I said, "All right. You're here, real or not. What do you want? *Why* are you here?"

He frowned and there was a deep rumble I realized was a thoughtful, "Hmm…" Then his face cleared. "Ah…I have to tell yiz something. A message."

"A message?"

"Aye, let me see… Ah, yes. You're a changeling."

"I'm a *what*?"

"A changeling. You was changed at birth."

I spread my hands, shaking my head, moving my mouth, trying to form any one of a thousand questions I wanted to ask.

Not one went beyond phonemes. "Wha…?" and "B…!"

He was grinning now, showing the tombstones he had for teeth, and raised a finger. "See, the *real* Jake Norgard is now living in Tír na nÓg, and you are living here with his human parents."

Somehow the words spilled out. "What are you *talking* about? *Human* parents? And where the hell is teernan… whatever?"

"Oh, Tír na nÓg is the land of the eternally young. Ti's over yonder. West, in another dimension of time and space. It's the land of the fairy folk. Tall fairies, small fairies, leprechauns, gnomes like my good self… And you yourself belong to the tall fairies—the elven folk—hence your dashing good looks and splendid figure, if I may say so."

"I'm a *fairy*? You are telling me I am a *fairy*? Are you *crazy*?"

"I told you. Only humans go crazy…on account of the boxes." He made the boxes movements with his hands. "But your mother and father are very fine, beautiful elven folk. And Jake is very happy with them. A fine lad…for a human."

My mind was reeling. "So, what? My mom and dad aren't my mom and dad? I-I'm a…what? I'm an orphan? I'm… like, *adopted*? They just gave me up? Why?"

He laughed mildly. "Isn't it the crazy capers of fairy folk? They do love a jape. Swap a child here, drain the blood from a cow there. Always up to some mischief. No telling *what* they'll do next."

I felt hollow. I went quiet then I said, "You're telling me my parents swapped me for another child for kicks? For a laugh?"

He sighed. "Fairies will be fairies." He could see I was upset and leaned forward to place one of his massive, gnarled hands on my shoulder. "Ah, don't be upset, lad. Don't your human parents love you? They don't know you're a changeling, by the way."

"I guess..."

"Sure, and it's not all bad. In compensation, in your seventeenth year, you come in to your powers."

"My powers?"

"That's right, lad. Your *powers!*"

Powers. Powers is one of those words that has a nice ring to it.

So, maybe I was given up by supernatural birth parents I had never known, but I was thinking that, from what I remembered of my mom, I wouldn't have swapped her for any mother in the world. And my dad was about as cool as dads get. And powers... If I wasn't going crazy and this crap was real, powers would be very cool. Actually, I was thinking about how I could use those powers to woo Ciara.

I said, "Powers? What powers?"

He stood. It was like talking to an office building. "First," he said, "you shall be invincible."

"Invincible? *Cooool!*" I could already see myself knocking seven bells out of Brutus Muller while Ciara looked on in awe.

Then Gorm said, "Aye! Invincible...with a sword."

"With a *sword*? Are you kidding? Nobody uses a sword anymore. What use is that power to me, Gorm?"

"Sorry, lad. I'm just the messenger. Your second power... and you'll like this. This is grand as aught." He chuckled. "All your arrows shall fly true to their mark. Is that grand or what?"

I sighed and rolled my eyes. "Great! I can be the archery champion of the world. Have you got anything *useful* in your bag of tricks?"

He scowled at me. "Ungrateful little fecker." Then his face lit up. "Ah, now! You'll like this one. Many a man has made his fortune with this one. This is a grand thing and no mistake."

I eyed him. *'Made his fortune'* sounded good. I said, "Go on. Lay it on me. What is it?"

"You shall be able to read any person's mind at will by simply concentrating on them. How's that for a power, eh? How's *that?*"

I covered my face with my hands. "Are you kidding me, Gorm? That is totally immoral. You can't go around spying on people's minds. What is wrong with you? That is so totally not cool, man."

"Jaysus! Is there no feckin' pleasin' you?"

"Not with powers that haven't been useful for half a millennium or are totally immoral. No! Is there anything else? Anything useful?"

"There may be, but I don't remember, if I'm perfectly honest. My memory isn't what it used to be."

"I know, you're three thousand years old—give or take. I can't fly or turn invisible?"

"Don't be daft."

I sighed. I felt suddenly dejected. "Is there at least some cool quest I get to go on? Find a crystal or save a princess? Take a ring to the Cracks of Doom?"

He looked at me like I was crazy. "No... Why would you?"

"So, this was just a laugh. My parents thought it would be a gas to swap me."

"That's about the size of it, lad. Now, if you'll excuse me, I must be getting along, as it seems you have no ale."

There was a flash of green light. I heard a weird, high-pitched shout, and suddenly, I was alone. For a few seconds I felt a burning on my chest but it passed, then there was just the silence of the dusk and the long, complicated song of the blackbird on the chimney.

I stared a long time at the garden bench. *Did it happen? Was it real? Did I hallucinate? Did I, in fact, have a psychotic break?* Maybe it had just been a dream. I glanced at my watch. September evenings in England are very long and the twilight lasts for hours. Even so, I was astonished to see that it was a quarter to nine. I had been sitting there for *four* hours.

I stood and made my way back. Through the open French windows, I could see the house was dark, but as I stepped in, the light in the hall came on. Then there was Rosie's voice, and my dad's, calling me. I stood waiting. Rosie's silhouette filled the doorway and the light snapped on.

"Jake? Are you okay? What are you doing here in the dark?"

I pointed back, out, through the open windows. "I was in the garden...listening to the blackbirds."

She frowned then smiled. "How sweet."

Dad pushed past her, laughing. "Next you'll be writing poetry. Run up and get washed, son. Dinner in half an hour. Martini, Rosie?"

As I passed her, she put a hand on my chest. I looked down and was surprised to see the three top buttons of my shirt were open and there was a medallion hanging around my neck. She smiled at me. "That's nice. I've never seen it before." Then she gave me a wink and walked past me, saying, "Yes please, darling. Nice and dry."

I peered at the medallion and held it in my fingers. She wasn't the only one who'd never seen it before. It appeared to be a couple of Nordic runes. It also had an inscription on the back. It said, "To my darling son, a gift from the gods. I am with you forever."

Then I remembered that high-pitched shout I'd heard as Gorm had disappeared, and I realized what it was. It was him, the great fool, shouting, "Jaysus! I forgot this."

A medallion — from my real mother.

Chapter Three

I didn't sleep that night. Any hope of convincing myself the whole thing had been a dream or a hallucination had been shattered by the medallion. I couldn't find a comfortable position in the bed. Whichever way I tossed or turned, the position was wrong, and I just couldn't silence my mind. To cap it all, it was a full moon and that pale, almost turquoise misty light filtered through the window and seemed to whisper or sing in my ear.

One minute, I was on fire with excitement. I was an elf, for crying out loud. And the best archer in the world, like Legolas! How damn cool was that? I saw myself joining the archery club and wowing every chick in town with my skill. And secretly knowing I was of elven descent, I would carry with me a certain charisma of mystery.

And I was an invincible swordsman. I turned, punched my pillow and gazed at the translucent moonlight. *An invincible swordsman.* That also was pretty cool. I could join the fencing club, become an unbeaten legend, maybe go into the movies. Again, the air of mystery…money, fame, women…

I turned over the other way. Outside, an owl hooted. Somewhere, far off in the ancient night of Albion, a fox cried out—if it was a fox. A deep knot of sadness twisted my gut. I didn't remember much about my mom. I did remember that she was beautiful. The photographs Dad kept of her proved that. She was petite and had the face of an angel. I also remembered she was sweet and kind and gentle. Dad said everybody loved her for that. I thought of the medallion and bit back a lump in my throat. The inscription should have been written by her, but it wasn't, because she wasn't my real mother. A wave of desolation swept over me. They had given me up as a laugh—as a joke.

And Dad. I had always admired my dad. He was cool— always happy, always calm, always had a solution to any problem. He was the rock of Gibraltar. He was my role model, and I wasn't ashamed to admit it. They had each been a kind of touchstone for me. And it was hard, real hard, to swallow the fact that they weren't my parents. Somewhere out there was the real Jake Norgard. *Will the real Jake Norgard please step forward…to claim my parents?*

* * * *

The next morning I got up feeling like the empty half of a glass half-empty. Bitter and twisted was the way I was going to feel when I started to feel better. Rosie was quiet on the way to school, for which I was grateful. I eyed her sidelong a couple of times, thinking that she wasn't even my stepmom anymore.

On the way through the doors, Ciara passed me and gave me a small smile that meant absolutely nothing. I made eye contact but managed to do absolutely nothing with my face, which I chalked up as a triumph. Score one to Jake the elf. *Treat 'em mean and keep 'em keen.* I wrenched open my locker and hurled in my bag, slammed and locked the door then marched off toward my first class of the day. Then I had to march back to get my books, and halfway through digging them out of my bag realized I had no idea what class I was attending or what books I needed. What was worse was I didn't care.

"I do believe you're in a funk, old chap."

I scowled up. I suddenly resented his damned equanimity, his cool, his confidence. Suddenly it looked to me like complacent self-satisfied arrogance. I said, "Are you always this cool, Sebastian? Don't you ever get mad, or pissed, or bitter?"

"Not often, no. By the way, pissed means something else in England."

"I don't care. I don't know what damned class I'm in. I'm pissed and I don't want to be here."

"Bad night?"

I snapped around and stared at him. "How do you know that?"

"I warned you it was unwise to fall in love. Check your timetable."

"What?"

"To see what books you need. Check your timetable. It's there, on the front of your folder."

I glared at the folder and the schedule like it was their fault I hadn't seen them before and began to grab my books. I felt his hand on my shoulder.

"Catch you at break, old boy. Chin up."

First and second period dragged on for an eternity. I didn't register a single word the teachers said and earned myself a severe reprimand from Miss Rowbotham, which she pronounced 'row-bottom' — and the best response I could muster was to think, sourly, what a stupid name she had.

Then, at eleven-thirty, everything changed — forever.

I had signed up for the baseball team. It was a decision I was regretting, because I knew Brutus Muller was bound to be on the team and I wanted to avoid him almost as much as I was beginning to want to avoid Ciara Fionn. And it was exactly those two people I saw in the corridor on my way to the changing rooms. Ciara was backed up against the wall and didn't look happy. Brutus was leaning over her, one hand against the wall on either side of her head. He was leering down at her. DB was there, laughing, and there were two or three other guys laughing, too. I guessed they were more of his cronies.

I felt my belly burning, but that sour voice that had been with me all day was telling me, "It's none of your business, Jake. Walk on and don't get involved. She belongs to him.

And, anyway, she thinks he's cute and funny, right?"

But as I drew closer, I could see by her face that she didn't think he was cute and funny anymore. She looked pretty angry and her green eyes were sparkling in a way that was anything but ambiguous. She was as annoyed as a long-tailed cat in a room full of rocking chairs. I heard her whisper, "Leave me *alone!*"

Brutus was saying, "Come on, baby. You know you want to. Give big old Brutus a little kiss…"

The stupid voice in my head told me she probably *did* want to, then followed up with something unprintable about what they could both go and do. The voice had moved on to how you could never trust anybody in this world and how girls and women would always let you down in the end, when Brutus took hold of her face with his hand and bent down to kiss her. The hot pellet in my belly turned into a raging fire just as Ciara let out an inarticulate shout and slapped his face. I do believe, in that moment, I felt true joy.

I stopped and watched Brutus' face turn crimson. His eyes bulged and his right hand swung for a backhander that would have knocked Ciara into late next week. I heard my own voice, loud and clear, ringing down the oak-paneled corridor, and Brutus froze.

"I wouldn't do that, Brutus—not if you want to walk out of this school on your feet this afternoon."

There was absolute silence. His face was a picture. He turned his head slowly to peer at me.

I said, "You heard what she said, ape man. The lady wants you to leave her alone."

I guess there is only so much a spoiled brat can take in a short period of time, and in a matter of a few seconds, Brutus had gone way beyond that limit. He turned his whole body now to face me, incredulity and rage wrestling for control of his ugly face.

"Did you speak to me, little man?" He looked around at his wingman, gaping theatrically. "Am I going crazy? Did this pipsqueak just *talk to me?*"

I knew what I was doing was stupid. In fact, what I was doing made stupid appear like Leonardo da Vinci on a serotonin high, but I didn't give a damn. All I could see right then was that the whole damned world was so damned unfair, and it was all, somehow, Freddy-damned-Brutus-damned-Muller's fault. And the small part of my brain that still retained some intelligence watched and listened in horror as I said, real loud, "What's the matter with you, Freddy? Are you deaf as well as stupid? The lady told you to leave her alone. And now I'm telling you to get lost before I do something you'll regret. Beat it!"

Whatever was going to happen next was worth it a thousand times over, just for the pleasure of seeing the expression on his face. More than that, for the one on Ciara's face, just behind him. Her eyebrows were arched high on her forehead, and her amazing green eyes were sparkling like the Mediterranean on a clear, spring morning.

It took him three strides to reach me. The backhander knocked me off my feet, made my ears ring and stung. When I opened my eyes, I saw three things through the ache in my head. First, I saw DB holding Ciara. She was struggling and trying to run either to me or at Brutus. She was shouting something I couldn't hear. Second, I saw Brutus turn and hold out his hand as someone threw him a baseball bat. He straddled me with his legs. He seemed to catch the bat in slow motion, turn to leer at me and mouth, "Get up, little man."

And third, I saw Sebastian stepping out of the changing rooms. He appeared as cool and impassive as ever. He was holding another baseball bat. He swung it and I watched it sail through the air toward me, slow and graceful.

I'll never know how I did it. I caught it by the handle, and the next thing I knew, I was on my feet, holding the bat as I would a saber, with my left hand relaxed behind my back. I smiled and heard myself, like I was somebody else, saying, "Last chance, Godzilla. Walk away."

He came at me, swinging the bat in a wide arc. If it had

connected, it would have knocked my head off. But he telegraphed it so far in advance that I would have had time to go home, read the paper, have a second breakfast and mow the lawn before coming back to parry the blow. The block jarred him to the bone and I stepped forward and placed the tip of the bat on his nose.

I said, "Lesson one, proto-man, do not slash. Thrust!" and I lunged forward, sending him staggering back, clutching at his nose with tears streaming down his face.

I gave the bat a couple of easy swings with my wrist, just for effect. "What's next, Oddjob?"

He hurled himself at me like an elephant on speed trying to swat a mosquito with an adrenaline overdose. All I could hear was his grunting and the rush of air as his bat swung past my head over and over again or smashed against my own bat—that, and my growing laughter as I ducked, parried and danced around him. I was, as Gorm had promised, invincible. He couldn't touch me.

Finally, he stopped, panting, with beads of sweat running down his face, and that was when I got serious. I fixed him with my eye and saw a glimmer of fear in his. "My turn, Gothmog…."

It was a dazzling display of skill and sheer brilliance. I sprang, and with perfect control, smashed my bat against his fingers. His bat clattered to the floor. Two sideswipes connected with his forearms, making him clutch at them in a self-embrace. I spun the bat in my hand, crouched and hammered his shins in two lightning-fast, devastating blows. As he staggered back, whimpering with pain, I leaped, jabbed him hard in the solar plexus and, as he doubled up, whiplashed his nose. His legs buckled and he collapsed to his knees.

I stepped up and placed the tip of the bat on his forehead. I cocked my head and said, "You're on your knees, Brutus. That is a perfect position from which to apologize to the lady. Do it."

It must have been hard for him. He actually wept before

he could say the words, but he said them. Really, he whispered them, so I made him say them again, louder.

"I'm sorry, Ciara."

Then, out of sheer devilry—I *am*, after all, a mischievous elf—I said, "On your back, ape man!" and I shoved. He fell, sprawling onto his back. I pointed the bat at him then at DB, who immediately let go of Ciara. "Do *not* touch the lady again, dogs, lest you incur the wrath of Norgard!"

It was a kind of a weird thing to say, I guess, but nobody laughed and it seemed to fit the occasion.

Brutus and his pack shuffled away to the changing rooms. Ciara looked at me with a weird expression I couldn't interpret then hurried away down the corridor. Sebastian was leaning against the wall, the way Englishmen do, with one leg crossed over the other, frowning at me.

He said, "Well, that was surprising."

I looked down at the bat. I couldn't help smiling, but I felt confused and suddenly very alone. I said, "Yeah..." I had to agree.

"Where did you learn to do that?"

"It's a long story." I couldn't meet his eye.

"I'd like to hear it."

"Some other time." I pointed over my shoulder with my thumb. "I think I'm going to resign from the baseball team, maybe join the fencing club."

"Admirable idea, I should say. Catch you at lunch?"

I nodded, threw him the bat and left.

* * * *

At lunchtime, I wasn't hungry, so instead of going to the Luncheon Hall, I went out into the gardens and sat under a large oak tree to think. I knew I was being a dork. My biological parents had given me up at birth. That sucked. But it only sucked if you knew it. And until yesterday I hadn't known it and I had been happy. What had changed apart from my knowledge? *Nothing!* What had changed

27

was me — my attitude.

I was lucky. I was lucky I had been given to two parents who loved me unconditionally. Sure, my mom had died, but the memories I had of her were beautiful, happy ones. My dad was as much a friend as he was my father. And he *was* my father, biological or not. I was lucky to have the life I had been given. The truth was there were plenty of kids in the world who had lost a lot more than their biological parents.

I smiled. Okay, I smiled ruefully, but I smiled. I was the best swordsman in the world — and the best archer! How cool was that? I should be grateful and overjoyed. And yet...I sighed — yes, I sighed ruefully — because even though this amazing thing had happened to me, the fact was I had no one I could share it with. For all that Dad was as much a friend as a father, for all that my mother had been the coolest mom in the world, there was no one on Earth I could tell about what had happened to me. They'd think I was crazy, and who could blame them? I'd thought I was crazy myself till I'd seen the medallion.

"Jake?"

I turned. It was Ciara. She smiled. It was an uncertain smile, but her eyes still looked like the Mediterranean with the morning sun on it.

I said, "Hi."

She hesitated, seemed to study my face then shrugged. "I just wanted to say thanks. It was pretty brave, what you did. And pretty amazing at the end." She gave a really cute laugh. I swallowed, coughed, blushed and prayed she hadn't noticed. She seemed not to and carried on. "I'm sorry you got hit, though."

I shrugged and tried to find my voice in all the turmoil inside my chest. It came out a bit mangled and I heard myself say, "With some people, it's whales or the environment. With me, it's Ciara Fionn." I wondered what the hell I was talking about and grinned stupidly.

She seemed like she thought I was insane but amusing

and she sat next to me. I noticed she had nice legs and I flushed again.

She said, "Is that what I am? A cause? Now that I'm rescued, will you lose interest?"

I was lost for words and had to turn away. I picked up a twig and examined it. Finally, I said, "Whales and the environment were both amazingly beautiful long before they became causes."

She laughed. I despaired.

She said, "You have a touch of the old blarney, so you have. Are you sure there isn't a touch of Irish in you?"

I joked, "Would you believe me if I told you I had a twin brother in Tír na nÓg?"

She seemed to study me for a moment. "I would at that. There's something of the Tuatha about you."

"Of the what? The two-ah?"

"Tuatha Dé Danann." She made it sound like two-ah de Danan. "The tribe of the goddess Danu — a kind of fairy folk from Irish mythology."

I must have stared, because she burst out laughing. Then I laughed, too, and I'm pretty sure there were bluebirds, a rainbow and a heavenly choir — but perhaps I just imagined that bit.

Anyway, after a while she put her hand on my shoulder and said, "Honest, Jake, thanks." She leaned over and gave me a kiss on the cheek. Then she was up and running across the grass.

I stammered a strangled, "Catch you around later..." after her and flopped back on the grass to grin like an idiot and relish the memory of her soft lips on my cheek.

In the midst of my bliss, something solid landed on my belly and Sebastian's voice said, "I brought you a disgusting sandwich."

I shaded my eyes and looked up at him as he sat down.

He added, "No need to thank me. I'd do the same for any miserable wretch."

I sat up and grinned at him. "You brought me a disgusting

sandwich and called me a miserable wretch. How could I not thank you?"

"She kissed you."

"How can you tell?"

"Quite aside from the fact that you have an idiotic grin on your face, I saw it."

"I think she likes me. She said I have blarney and I look like a Tuatha."

"Oh, good grief."

"Come on. Let's go have some real food. I'm starving."

"Oh, good *grief!*"

On the way in to the Luncheon Hall, we didn't talk much, but I couldn't shake the feeling that, though this was a guy I hardly knew, in this short time he had become a friend. He'd reached out a hand when he'd known I was in trouble, even though he had no idea what trouble I was in. I also had the feeling that if I didn't tell somebody about what had happened to me, I was going to go crazy. And what are friends for, right, if not to stop you going crazy?

The Luncheon Hall was fairly crowded when we got in. We grabbed some food and found a place to sit. I saw Brutus and his pals just a couple of benches away. They ignored us, but they were looking pretty sheepish. Sebastian started cutting at his steak and kidney pie. He was quiet. I knew he was giving me space and time to tell him what was troubling me. I picked up my knife and fork, took a deep breath and set them down again.

"Sebastian?"

"Yes, old chap?"

"I have something I need to share with you."

"Fire away. I'm all ears."

"I don't really know how to say this."

He frowned at me with a forkful of food halfway to his mouth. "Just plunge in. Start at the beginning and go from there."

Just plunge in. Okay. "You're not going to believe me, but here goes." I leaned forward and lowered my voice. "You see, the thing is, Sebastian, I am a fairy."

You have to admire the English stiff upper lip. His only reaction was to raise his left eyebrow. He swallowed, dabbed his mouth with his napkin and smiled at me. "I am a little surprised, after your carry on with Ciara. But though I don't share your proclivity personally, these days it is nothing to be ashamed of. Have you spoken to your parents?"

"No, you don't understand. My dad isn't my biological father —"

"You think it might have a Freudian root? Still, Jake, there is not the stigma attached to it these days. I would honestly just come out with it, if you'll excuse the pun."

"Will you stop? I am trying to tell you. I am not a normal person. I'm an *actual* fairy."

He sighed. "Look, Jake. I hate to burst your bubble, but it really is not a big deal anymore."

"Will you cut it out already? I am trying to tell you, me and all my family are *fairies*! My dad, my mom... Every one of us *is. A. Fairy!*"

There was a deathly silence as my voice echoed around the Luncheon Hall. Sebastian sat blinking at me and wiping his mouth as heads turned to stare at me. There was a loud clatter of a tray hitting the floor and Brutus rose to his feet and slammed out of the room, followed by DB.

Suddenly Sebastian burst out laughing. People glanced at each other and shrugged and turned back to their meals. Sebastian spread his hands. "I really don't know what you want me to say, Jake. It isn't an issue for me."

I sighed. I realized he thought I was saying I was gay. "Let me start again. Racially, ethnically, genetically, I am not human. I am of the fairy folk. I am an elf, if you like. I am a changeling. I was swapped at birth. I am not human. Don't worry. I don't expect you to believe me, but I only found out yesterday and needed to tell somebody."

"I'm flattered. May I urge you not to tell anybody else?"

"I don't intend to. I didn't believe it myself at first, but then I saw the medallion."

"Medallion?"

"It's a long story. I realize I can't expect you to believe it. I have to prove it to you. I get that."

"Jake, before we go any further, you have to realize that this is a delusion. It isn't real. It happens sometimes, but these days it is treatable."

"I'm not crazy, Sebastian. I can prove it. Listen, I have *never* done fencing or any kind of sword fighting *in my life!* I have never shot a bow, but I'm going to join the archery club and you'll see. I won't miss a single shot. I'll split an arrow for you. I'll split five! Ten!"

He sighed and drummed his fingers on the table. "So being an elf means you can automatically use a sword and shoot a bow?"

I shook my head. "Uh-uh, these are my gifts. The powers I was given."

"To help you get the ring to Mount Doom."

"No, there is no quest."

"Jake, listen to yourself. You really need to talk to your father about this and get help."

"Wait! I *can* prove it to you."

He appeared pained and sighed loudly. "How? You going to take me for a walk on a rainbow?"

"I can read your mind. I was given three gifts — maybe more, but that isn't important now — and the last one was that I can read people's minds. Will you give me permission to read yours?"

Now he seemed bored. He spread his hands. "Be my guest."

I closed my eyes and concentrated. "Okay, you're a bit disappointed and embarrassed, because you thought I was a nice guy, but this is getting a bit too weird and now you want a polite, diplomatic way to get out."

I opened my eyes. He was watching me. He said, "You don't need to be a mind reader to see that, Jake."

I held up my hands. "Okay, wait..." I closed my eyes

again and tried to go deeper into his mind. Then I said, "Sarah. Sarah Churchill."

"What?"

I opened my eyes. He was serious. I said, "Sarah Churchill. You were crazy about her last year. You still are. You never really got over her, but she left you. She left you for...Nigel. Nigel Weller, the captain of the rugby team. She said... She said you were too nice."

He screwed up his paper napkin and dropped it on his plate. He had his lips in a tight line. He said, "Not funny, Jake. Not funny. Sorry." He stood up. "Don't get too clever, Jake. It's liable to backfire on you sooner or later."

"No, wait."

"Goodbye, Jake."

He walked away. I tried to call after him, "Wait. You don't understand!" A few heads turned, but he didn't. He just walked away, out of the Luncheon Hall.

I looked down at my food. I hadn't touched it. And I'd lost my appetite again.

"Shit!"

Chapter Four

I spent the rest of the day in a weird agony of mixed feelings. I was buzzing and elated because I knew in my bones that Ciara liked me. At the same time, I felt like crap because I had upset Sebastian, and in a short time, I had come to think of him as a friend. He was one of the good guys, and I was afraid I'd blown our friendship. What made it worse was that I had been disgusted when Gorm had given me the power to read other people's minds precisely because it was an invasion of their privacy and I'd gone and done just that with Sebastian, trampling all over his most private feelings, just to prove a point.

The next couple of days dragged by and were anticlimactic. I hardly saw Ciara except a couple of times in the distance — usually running to get in her dad's Jag — and she made zero effort to see me or talk to me. In fact, she seemed to be trying to avoid me. I did see Sebastian a few times, but when I tried to talk to him, he cut me dead with an empty smile as he walked straight past me.

One minute, it had seemed like I had the girl of my dreams, the best pal a guy could ask for, plus these amazing powers, and in a matter of a few seconds, those very powers had cost me my friend, and the girl of my dreams seemed to have forgotten I even existed.

That was Tuesday and Wednesday, but on Thursday, things began to look up. As I was no longer on the baseball team, I had joined the fencing club and the archery club. The archery club was on Thursday afternoons, and on Wednesday, I'd gone with Rosie to buy a nice six-foot yew longbow with a fifty-pound draw weight and a dozen wooden arrows. The guy at the shop had tried to sell me a carbon fiber beginner's bow with a twenty-pound draw weight, but I'd told him I was an experienced archer and wanted a pro bow. I'd glanced at Rosie when I'd said it because I'd thought she might have something to say about that, but she'd just smiled at me and paid the thousand pounds without batting an eyelid.

I decided Rosie was cool.

So, on Thursday, I stood on the green with my bow and arrows, a mere thirty yards from the target, while the instructor sighed and shook his head, peering at my longbow. "Don't get me wrong," he said. "It's a lovely bow. A real craftsman made this. But it is a professional bow. It's very hard to draw fifty pounds, and on a bow like this, you have no sights, no aids...nothing. I mean, you'll hardly be able to draw it, let alone hit the target. Let me lend you a beginner's bow."

I shook my head. "If it's all the same to you, I'd like to learn on this one. It's the kind of bow I plan to use in the future, so even if it takes a while..."

He shrugged and, with a touch of irony, said, "Suit yourself, but if you change your mind, just let me know." He said it like he knew that in five minutes I'd be coming to him with my tail between my legs. Then he said, "Now, do you know how to string it?"

I smiled. "String it?"

He sighed and showed me how, which on a fifty-pound bow is not easy. The wood is so hard to bend that you have to wedge it between your legs. I was beginning to fear he might be right. Then he showed me how to hold it, how to nock the arrow—fit it to the string—how to draw, how to aim and, finally, how to loose. "Incidentally," he added, "you 'loose' an arrow or you shoot an arrow. You don't fire it. There is no gunpowder involved." He smiled at me like I was a little backward but sweet all the same, then he handed me the bow. "Have a try..."

I took hold of the bow like he'd said, and it was as though

my body took over. All I did was watch myself do something I didn't even know I could do. I nocked the arrow and, in one swift, easy movement, I drew, using my back instead of my arms, and loosed, and in a fraction of a second, the arrow was shuddering at the center of the bullseye.

I grinned at him. "Beginner's luck?"

He stared at the arrow. "That was perfect. Are you having a laugh at my expense?"

I promised him I wasn't, but he didn't believe me. I shot a couple more times and when it was clear it wasn't beginner's luck, he moved me to the most difficult targets at a hundred yards, muttering something about 'clever dickheads'.

I spent a happy half-hour making pretty patterns with the placing of my arrows. I was constantly amazed that, wherever I put my eye, that was where the arrow went. I made pentagrams, hexagons, flowers, crosses...you name it. I'd even choose frayed bits of straw between the colored bands on the target and hit them dead on. Just the feeling of loosing the arrows and knowing they would fly true to the mark was exhilarating. I could have spent all day doing it.

It was after about half an hour, I had just placed my arrow in the bullseye and was drawing my second, when there was a whisper of air and suddenly my barb had been split down the middle and a second arrow was quivering at the middle of my target. I turned and Ciara was standing next to me, holding a bow that was almost identical to mine.

She smiled and said, "Oops, wasn't that a little careless of me?"

I think I blinked a lot, and the most blarney thing I could manage was, "Ciara!"

She frowned and said, "Are you stalking me?"

"No! I didn't even know you did arch—"

"I seem to run into you an awful lot for someone I'm trying to avoid."

My stomach lurched and I spread my hands. "Why are you trying to avoid me?"

She pulled and loosed in one fluid movement and hit

dead center. "It's complicated."

I also pulled and loosed in one fluid movement and split the arrow she'd put in my target down the middle. "How complicated? Have you got a jealous boyfriend?"

"God, no!" She glanced at me as though I were crazy and I felt a warm glow all over. "No, it's much worse than that."

"Like what?"

She sighed and looked down at her bow. "I'm not in the mood for this today. Do you fancy a drink?"

"Sure!"

We bought a couple of fruit juices in cartons and sat on the grass. I said, "I don't believe you want to avoid me. I know we hit it off."

"It's my dad. He's a bit— He's *very* over-protective."

"Why would he have a problem with me? I protected you."

She cocked her head. "Come on! You're *exactly* the kind of boy he wants to protect me against. It's not *me* he's protecting. It's himself and what he sees as his property." We sat in silence a moment while I nodded. Then she added, "Besides, I could never tell him what happened. He'd kill me."

"He'd kill *you*? Surely, he'd want to kill Brutus!"

She laughed. "Are you joking? It would be my fault for not staying away from the bloody oaf!"

"That's harsh."

"He keeps me on a pretty tight rein."

"What about your mom?"

She gave a lopsided smile. "Yeah, she's not...*with* us."

"Sorry. I didn't mean to pry."

"It's okay. I don't mind telling *you*." She stressed the 'you' like she *would* mind telling somebody else. "I trust you, for some reason." We both laughed. It was nice and companionable.

"Listen..." She knew what I was going to say and I could see her face setting into a 'forget it' expression, but I pressed on, anyway. "Why don't we do something sometime?

We could go to the movies or take some bikes and have a picnic?"

She was already shaking her head. "I'd love to, Jake. Truly, I would, but there's no way my dad would let me."

"Come on. Tell him I'm gay. No, tell him I'm a girl. Tell him I'm a gay girl. No! Don't tell him that!"

We both started laughing and she put her hand on my knee. I put my hand on hers. She didn't take it away, and it was the most natural thing in the world. She drew breath to say no, but instead she said, "I'll tell you what. My dad has a boat. Our house is right on the banks of the Isis. He's away for the weekend and I'm alone with my nanny. There's a wee pier near my house. I'll pick you up there Saturday morning and we'll spend a couple of hours on the river. How's that?"

I beamed like an idiot. "It sounds perfect."

Her face became serious. "But, Jake, it isn't something we can do often. I'm" — she shrugged — "I'm not like other kids. My dad is…" She hesitated. "He's in politics. And he keeps a very tight hold on me. Do you understand?"

"Sure."

We were silent for a moment. Then she said, "I'd better go."

She stood and I scrambled to my feet after her. She shouldered her archery kit and I said, "But, Ciara?"

"Yes…"

"I don't give up easy. I won't stop trying."

She hesitated, not meeting my eye. Finally, she looked up and said, "Good."

And she was gone.

* * * *

If I thought I was hitting home run, I was sadly mistaken. At the risk of seriously confusing my metaphors, the helter-skelter had only just begun. When I got back to my house, Rosie was in the kitchen sipping a glass of wine while she made a steak pie. She grimaced at me as I came in and said, "Your dad wants to have a word with you. He's in his study." I made a question out of a frown but she shook her head and said, "Don't ask. You'd better just talk to him."

I found him sitting behind his big oak desk appearing troubled and unhappy. He waved his hand at a chair and said, "Sit down, son," but he wouldn't meet my eye.

I sat and said, "What is it, Dad?"

He picked up a piece of paper off his desk and stared at it a while. Finally, he said, "I've had this email from the headmaster of your school. He wants to meet with us, Jake, both you and me, tomorrow afternoon in his office."

I frowned. "What for?"

He raised his eyes to look at me. He appeared sad but mad as well. "There has been a complaint against you. You've been accused of beating up a boy. There are witnesses."

I sagged back in my chair. "Brutus. Freddy Muller. Of all the—"

"So, it's true?"

"No, Dad, it's not true! We *did* have a fight—sort of—but I didn't beat him up!"

"You had a fight. On your second day in your new school—"

"Dad, he was abusing a girl. He was forcing her to kiss him and she was struggling to get away. I had to do *something!*"

He was silent for a while, staring at me. He said, "So what did you do?"

"I told him to leave her alone."

"And?"

"He hit me. I fell to the ground and he was going to hit me with a baseball bat."

"So, what happened, son?"

"I defended myself."

He stared at me a long while. Then he waved the email at me. "The boy has a medical report from ER. He claims it says he was black and blue from head to toe. What did you do to him, son?"

"No..." I shook my head. "No, Dad... He was in the Luncheon Hall afterward. He was a bit bruised, but it was nothing."

"You are going to have to answer these charges, young man. One thing is helping a young lady who is in trouble. Quite another is sending a boy to the hospital. Go have your dinner, and tomorrow you had better have a damned good explanation for the headmaster. Because if you are expelled from this school, you are going to be in *big* trouble, mister."

Chapter Five

I spent the next day in a state of anxiety. I searched for Sebastian to ask him to be my witness for what had happened, but it turned out he hadn't come in that day because he had an interview at the university. I saw Ciara and she smiled at me, but we didn't talk. And in any case, I was determined that I was going to keep her out of the whole affair. The last thing she needed was her dad getting to hear about the incident.

Finally, at three p.m. my dad turned up and we went to Mr. Clarendon's office. When we arrived, Brutus was already there with DB. I was surprised to see that his father was not there. Mr. Clarendon stood, shook my dad's hand and said, "Thank you for coming, Mr. Norgard. Please, take a seat. You too, Jake." We sat and so did he, while Brutus watched us. I couldn't see any black and blue bruising, though his nose was a bit swollen.

Mr. Clarendon said, immediately, "Mr. Norgard, let me be very clear about this. As it stands, this meeting is quite simply to decide whether Jake stays at the Anglo-American school or whether he is expelled forthwith."

My dad's face darkened. "Mr. Clarendon, hadn't we better have a look at the allegation and at the evidence before we take any kind of—?"

"That is precisely what we are here to do," cut in Mr. Clarendon, "but I want to leave you in no doubt, Mr. Norgard, about the seriousness of the allegation against your son, or indeed, how seriously we take this kind of incident. Now, Mr. Muller, would you please tell us, according to you, what happened on Tuesday last?"

Brutus shifted in his seat and smirked at me. "Yes, sir, Mr. Clarendon. I was coming out of the changing rooms to go to the baseball grounds and I saw Jake here coming along the corridor towards me. I knew he was a new boy and, wishing to make him feel welcome, I greeted him. At which point he said to me, 'You're the captain of the football team, right?' To which I said I was, and he said, 'Well, get used to the fact that there's a new kid on the block.' At this point, he punched me in the solar plexus and winded me. Then I realized he was carrying a baseball bat and he laid into me with the bat around my chest, arms and legs. When I was on the floor and unable to move, he told me he would be taking over as captain and that I should stay out of his way."

I turned at Dad to see if he was swallowing this crock. He was frowning hard, but apart from that it was difficult to tell what he was thinking. He just said, "And you have a report from the hospital?"

Mr. Clarendon slid a sheet of paper across the desk for him to see, muttering, "I did email you a scan of the original…"

Dad glanced at it, but I could see it was the same document. He gave it back and said to Brutus, "Mr. Muller, I would like to see your bruises with my own eyes."

"Of course, Mr. Norgard." He stood up, pulled off his blazer and undid his shirt. His chest was a mass of bruises, and he had bruising on his arms, too. I knew I had not caused those bruises. It was impossible.

Dad and Mr. Clarendon both turned to peer at me.

Dad said, "What have you got to say for yourself, son?"

I looked Dad in the eye then Mr. Clarendon. When I heard my voice, it was weird. It was like I was listening to somebody else talking. "Mr. Clarendon. I will tell you exactly what happened. But before I do, I want to say that I did *not* cause those bruises. I have no idea where they came from, but I do know that I didn't cause them."

Dad was frowning. He said, "Go ahead, son."

"In the corridor outside the dressing rooms, I came across

Freddy Muller, Darren Engles and a couple of other boys. Freddy had a girl pinned against the wall and he was trying to force her to kiss him. She was clearly distressed and telling him to leave her alone. When I saw what was happening, I told Freddy to let her go, at which point, he became angry and punched me to the ground. Then he got a baseball bat and prepared to beat me with it. I took another bat that was thrown to me by another boy. I am a very proficient fencer..." I glanced at Dad and tried hard to ignore his expression of astonishment. "I used the bat as I would use a saber and was able to defend myself, for which reason I am responsible for the slight swelling on Freddy's nose and some slight bruising you will find on his forearms and shins. But I am *not* responsible for those bruises." I pointed at his torso. "In fact, if you check the Luncheon Hall records, sir, you will find that he and DB — that is Darren Engles — had luncheon there shortly after the incident, which he would not have been able to do if he had been at the hospital."

Dad and Mr. Clarendon were silent, staring at the floor.

I said, "I would also like to add an observation, sir, if I may. Comparing our relative sizes and taking into account the fact that Freddy is the captain of the football team, it is very unlikely that I would have been able to inflict that kind of bruising on him."

Mr. Clarendon studied Brutus for a long while. Brutus looked like he was sitting on an angry ferret but didn't want to let on.

The headmaster turned back to me and said, "Who is this girl?"

I shook my head. "I am sorry, sir. I am not at liberty to say. Her part in this was that of an innocent victim, but if her father heard of it he would be very angry with her. I can't do that."

"You realize that without her testimony, you cannot substantiate your story."

"I do realize that, sir, and even so, I am afraid I can't bring her into it. But I would respectfully submit to you that Mr. Muller's story is sufficiently hard to believe to cast doubt on the whole incident he alleges. Furthermore, sir, I have joined the fencing and the archery clubs, I have pulled out of the baseball team and I haven't even joined the football team, which does not make much sense if I wanted to take over as captain. And the fencing club will vouch for my skill with a sword, sir."

He flopped back in his chair and stared at me. Brutus was going slowly crimson.

Mr. Clarendon said, "Apparently it isn't just a sword you have skill with. You are quite right. The whole incident is insufficiently clear for me to take any action. But you are both" — and he turned and raised a withering eyebrow at Brutus — "*both* on notice that if there is one more incident of this sort, clear or unclear, you will *both* be out on your ears. Am I understood?" We both muttered that he was and he turned to Brutus, "I don't know how you received those bruises, Mr. Muller, but I am satisfied that it was not from Mr. Norgard. So, you may be sure that I shall be watching you with interest from now on. You are dismissed." As Brutus got to his feet and left, Mr. Clarendon turned to me, "Not you, Mr. Norgard, though I shall also be watching you with interest. Who knows? You may yet be an asset to the school. I just hope I am not making a mistake. However, you get to stay, young man, but I want something in exchange."

I was surprised and so was my dad. "Yes, sir?"

He nodded. "You are eloquent and you think on your feet. I want you on the debating team. You have," he said, "the gift of the gab. I am quite serious. I want you on the debating team, winning trophies for us."

* * * *

We went down to the car in silence. Once we had climbed in and slammed the doors, my dad sat gazing at the steering wheel for a moment. Finally, he said, "You are a very proficient fencer? Since *when?*"

"I—"

"You have never picked up a sword in your life!"

"I… It just seemed to come to me naturally."

"You lied, Jake…"

I shook my head, "No, Dad, no I didn't!"

"You have never learned to fence, Jake!"

"I didn't say I had. I said I was proficient. And, Dad, ask at the fencing club! They'll tell you. I am really good." Then I added, "I wouldn't lie, Dad."

He sighed and shook his head. "I don't know what's going on, Jake, but I know that there is *something* that you are not telling me about. Now"—he stared hard at the wheel—"I'm sorry, Jake. I know you meant well, but you got into a fight in the corridor on your *second* day in school! That is *irresponsible!* You could have handled that in many different ways, and you chose to fight that boy. I have no choice. I'm sorry. You are grounded for the weekend."

I looked at him in horror. "No! Dad! No, no, no, you can't! Please, Dad. You don't understand. Not *this* weekend!"

He frowned at me. "Why? What's so special about this weekend?"

"I…" I flopped back in the seat and closed my eyes. "Dad, just…please, not this weekend."

I glanced over at him and he was smiling. "Who is she?"

I turned away. "I don't know what you mean."

"The girl Muller was trying to kiss and the girl you are supposed to be meeting this weekend. Who is she?"

I sighed. "Ciara Fionn."

He cocked his head. "Michael Fionn's daughter?"

I shrugged. "I guess. She said he's some kind of political figure."

"He's a leading consultant on environmental issues. He works for the European Commission. He's a gray suit, but he is a very powerful man."

He started the car and began to pull away.

I asked, "So can I see her?"

"Not this weekend, son." He eased into the traffic and accelerated. "I'm sorry. You have to learn that your actions have consequences, Jake. Take a rain check till next weekend."

"But, Dad —"

"It's final, Jake. No means no."

* * * *

That night over dinner the atmosphere around the table was tense. We ate in silence. I couldn't stop thinking that if I didn't see Ciara that weekend, it might be weeks before I got another chance. But after a while, I noticed that Rosie's face was rigid and she wouldn't raise her face from her plate. Dad kept glancing at her and appeared decidedly worried. Finally, she laid down her knife and fork and looked straight at him. Her face was not a reassuring sight.

"George, there is something I do not understand."

He smiled nervously, "Yes, honey?"

"As I understand it, your son took on the captain of the American football team, a young man of six foot six, built like the proverbial brick —"

"Yes, honey."

She paused, eying him sternly. "A very tall, powerfully built young man. Your son took him on, in spite of considerable risk to himself, in order to defend a young lady who was being molested by this lout. A lout who is also, by all accounts, the school bully."

Dad smoothed his hair and loosened his collar.

Rosie turned to me and said, "Is that right, Jake?"

I looked at Dad and said, "Pretty much."

"So, your son," she went on, "behaved like a perfect gentleman with admirable courage, and is now, no doubt, Ciara Fionn's knight in shining armor. And for this he is being punished?"

Dad sighed. "Rosie, it isn't that simple. You just can't go into a school like the Anglo-American and, on your second day, start beating up another kid – even if he *is* the captain of the football team..."

"On the contrary, George, 'simple' is precisely the adjective I would use."

"Rosie, please, honey. Jake has to learn discipline, and he has to learn obedience. I'm sorry –"

She cut right across him. "I see. Well, thankfully, George, rather than this foolish, pseudo-military nonsensical claptrap you seem suddenly to be spouting, your son seems to have assimilated the values I have always admired so much in you when you are not trying to be General Westpoint Wally. And he has behaved exactly as I would hope *you* would have behaved in a similar situation – *not* according to the stupid rules of some fossilized institution but according to his own judgment and a heroic heart!"

"Um...Rosie, honey –"

"However" – she snapped out the word and it was like she'd slapped him across the face – "your father has made up his mind, and he is your father, so we have no choice but to abide by his decision, however reactionary and Stone Age it may seem to us. It is a shame, because I was going to take you both to see Stonehenge tomorrow. But now you won't be able to come. Your father and I shall go, Jake, and you will be left home alone. I hope you'll be able to use the time productively."

I swear she winked at me then. Dad didn't see because, as well as turning scarlet, he was staring so hard at his plate that he couldn't have seen anything but his food.

He said, "We're going to Stonehenge?"

"Yes then Avebury. It's fascinating, and I was really looking forward to showing Jake. They are among some of the most ancient, mystical places on the planet."

He glanced at me then back at Rosie. "Well, I guess, if it was educational –"

"Nope! You have decided and that's final. We can take Jake some other time."

She stood up, collected the plates and went out to the

47

kitchen. We stared at the table a second then we peered at each other.

He said, "What just happened?"

I shook my head. "I have no idea, Dad, but I can see why you're crazy about her."

He nodded then smiled. "Right."

I smiled back. "Yeah, enjoy Stonehenge."

"Right…"

Chapter Six

Ciara picked me up from the small jetty at about eleven the next morning in a small white rowing boat. She was wearing denim shorts and a white blouse, and the sun was dancing on her hair. She had her back to me as she was rowing, but she paused to turn and wave, and her smile was everything I could have wanted it to be. What Rosie had said... She was smiling at her knight in shining armor.

When she arrived, she had a picnic basket with sandwiches, drinks and a basket of strawberries in it. I laughed when I saw it and showed her the one I'd brought along. It was almost identical.

"Well," she said, winking at me, "I'll have yours and you can have mine."

"Sounds like a deal to me."

I don't remember what we talked about. It wasn't really important. I think we spent a lot of time not talking, just looking at each other and smiling — or maybe not even smiling. I never felt so comfortable or so happy as I did sitting in that boat, just watching her gently pull on the oars with the sun on her hair and her green eyes smiling at me.

I know she talked about the birds and that was bewitching, because she spoke about them not like an expert but as though she knew them — each one — individually and personally, and I'm pretty sure she called some of them by name. When I think back, it was almost like a dream. I know she also talked about the fish in the same way, but hard as I tried, I couldn't remember the exact words she used.

Eventually, we came to a small island in the middle of the river and she eased in among reeds and weeping willows until the boat was invisible from the banks. Then we climbed out and tied the boat to the trunk of a tree. We ducked through some matted branches and came out in a clearing. In the middle, there was a ten-foot standing stone. The grass around it was slightly paler and shorter than the deep green grass in the rest of the clearing and there was an abundance of small daisies and clover.

She sat down cross-legged at the foot of the stone in a single, fluid movement and I sat opposite her. She held my eye, smiled and handed me her picnic basket. I took it and she held out both her hands for mine. I placed it in her hands and she appeared quietly pleased.

"We have exchanged food. That makes us friends."

"Weren't we friends before?"

She thought about it a moment then let go of my hand to open the hamper and look inside. "No, we wanted to be, but we weren't. But now" — she pulled out a large strawberry and bit into it — "we have defied the 'Laws That Be' for each other. You defied the school, I have defied my father and we have exchanged food. I think that makes us friends now."

I told her I had also defied my own father and explained what had happened at the school the day before. "Don't worry," I said. "I refused to give them your name. And Brutus didn't want you involved either, because you'd confirm my story."

She reached over and took my hand again. "I'm so sorry, Jake. You're so good to me, and you barely even know me." She suddenly giggled. "You're like a knight in shining armor or a fairy-tale prince, and all I give you in return is trouble."

I shook my head and kept hold of her hand. "Tell me about your dad. Why does he keep such a tight hold on you?" I smiled. "Not that I wouldn't like to have a tight hold on you myself from time to time."

She gave my hand a gentle smack. "Behave, Mr. Norgard." Then she became serious. "Jake, I think I should get this over with as soon as possible. You need to know. You *deserve* to know."

My heart gave a sick jolt. I said, "You already told me you haven't got a boyfriend."

She raised her eyes to Heaven, but she kept hold of my hand. "If only it were that simple, Jake. Sure, all I'd have to do is leave him."

My heart gave another jolt, but of a different type this time.

"It's a lot more complicated than that. There are things about me that you can never know — things I can never tell you. I really like you, Jake. I do. I feel something special, hard to explain…"

"I feel the same, Ciara."

"But what *I* feel and what *I* want just don't come into it. Whatever I might feel, we can never be anything more than friends — and even that is pushing it."

"What kind of things, Ciara?"

She laughed out loud and reached out her free hand to hold mine with both of hers. "Well, that would be telling you, wouldn't it?"

I studied her face. She looked real sad but resigned. I had no doubt in my mind from that moment on that she felt the same as I did, but there was an obstacle in her life — something that I had to shift out of the way.

I said, "Is it your dad?"

She shrugged. We were right up close now, with our knees touching, holding each other's hands. "He doesn't help, but he isn't the problem. He's the way he is partly because of the problem."

A terrible thought struck me. "Are you ill? Is that it? Because I don't care. I'll do anything…"

"No, Jake! No, no, it isn't that. I'm not ill." She drew breath and closed her eyes. "I-I would so love to tell you, of all people, because for some reason, I trust you in my heart. But I can't. It's no good."

I thought for a second longer, staring down at her hands

51

and stroking her fingers with my thumbs. They were long and fine. I could imagine her playing the harp. Finally, I said, "I also have a secret." I looked up and held her eyes with mine. "It's a pretty crazy secret. You probably wouldn't even believe it, but I'll tell you if you tell me yours."

She let go of my hand and touched my cheek, and there were tears in her green eyes that made them shine like emeralds.

"I can't."

I heard my words and it was like another me was talking through me, from far, far away. "Ciara, whatever it is, however impossible, I swear to you that I will overcome it. There will come a day when there are no secrets between us. You know that, in your heart."

She was quiet a long while, while she touched my face with her fingers. Eventually her face cleared and she changed her expression and smiled as though she had just seen me for the first time and was happy. "My knight in shining armor. My prince." And she leaned forward and so softly that it was the gentlest, sweetest thing I had ever felt in my life, she placed her lips on mine and kissed me.

Next, it was like waking from a dream with a violent start. There was a wild rushing of a thousand wings. The air seemed to go crazy, like a tornado had hit us out of nowhere. Above the flapping and the turbulent air there was a wild screeching and twittering. I looked up and saw that the sky our heads had gone black with a huge, dense cloud of birds of all sizes and shapes. There were a million starlings, finches, robins, blackbirds, ravens and even seagulls whirling in a huge vortex just a few feet above us. And they were all screeching at the same time in a nightmarish cacophony.

Then Ciara was grabbing at my arm, shouting over the noise, "We have to *go*! We have to get out of here *now*!"

She stumbled to her feet, dragging me after her, knocking the hampers flying. I was shouting, "What the *hell* is going on?" But she ignored me and we crashed through the undergrowth back toward the dingy. As we pushed the boat back into the water, all I could hear was the crashing of the birds against the branches of the trees and their insane screaming. However, we were only a few feet into the water, so I tried battering at the trees to scare them off, but Ciara was grabbing at my arms, screaming at me, "Leave them *alone*! Leave them *alone*! Get in the boat!"

We heaved the boat into the river and leaped in. I grabbed the oars and she shouted at me, "Downstream! Go *downstream*!"

Then we were grabbed by the current and were easing past the island with the massive flock wheeling above us. I looked at her as I rowed and she was staring up at the birds, like she was scanning and listening to them.

I shouted again over the din, "*Ciara!* What the *hell* is happening?"

She stared at me wide-eyed, like her mind was racing and nothing she was thinking was anything she could say. Finally, she just mouthed, "Just row."

I heaved on the oars and, moving with the current, we began to pick up speed. The birds churned the air, making their terrible noise, but they didn't come any closer and they didn't touch us. They just held their distance while Ciara stared at them and seemed to scan the sky and the riverbanks beside us. I went to speak but she held up her hand, cocking her head from side to side, as though listening to something.

Then the river exploded. Ciara screamed. Two massive torrents of water erupted into the air, raining on us and rocking the small boat so violently that I thought it would capsize. I heaved on the oars, but the river was boiling so fiercely that we made no headway. Then the two vast columns of water collapsed and crashed down, drenching us to our skin. I pulled on the oars again, trying to make for the bank. Ciara was scrambling to sit next to me. Her hair was matted with water and she was wiping her eyes. She grabbed the right oar, I had the left then we froze, gaping, because we were staring at the things that had burst out of the river.

Hovering fifteen or twenty feet above us in the air were two vast yellow emoticons, smiling at us. The left one opened its mouth and a speech balloon appeared out of thin air. It said, "LOL." And as I stared at it, the right one changed. It suddenly had on a red bandana, an eye-patch and an arm had sprouted from its side holding a cutlass.

I screamed, "Row!" and we both worked the oars. The current seemed to have grown stronger and we were moving fast along the river with the giant emoticons speeding after us. The pirate was gaining, and as it approached, it raised the cutlass and slashed down, slicing into the water and missing us by inches.

Ciara glanced over her shoulder and shouted, "Tree cover! Your side! Twenty yards!"

I missed a pull so we swung to my side just as another swipe of the cutlass missed our stern, and we both shouted, "Heave! Heave! Heave!" as we pulled on the oars. We were approaching the trees and the second emoticon, who'd just been bobbing along till then, suddenly morphed into a hot-air balloon with purple and blue stripes. His yellow face leered out of the basket in an Austrian World War I spiked helmet. As my jaw dropped, he produced a spherical black bomb with a fuse and hurled it at us. It landed with a clatter at our feet in the row boat. I lunged for it, grabbed it with both hands and hurled it into the river. Behind me, Ciara was struggling for my oar.

I yelled, "Duck!" and there was another vast explosion of water that drenched us in torrents.

The boat was now half full of water. It was heavy, low and sluggish. The two emoticons, now two insanely grinning faces, opened their mouths and a shared speech balloon appeared with the letters, "LMAO!" As we pulled on the oars, inching under the tree cover toward the bank, they changed again, this time into two gigantic cartoon sharks. They plunged into the water, maybe forty feet away.

In unison, we shouted to each other as we heaved on the oars, "Pull! Pull! *Pull!*"

We heard the keel grind on the mud and grit of the shore and we leaped from the boat onto the sludge of the bank, just as the water erupted again and the two sharks smashed into the boat, ripping out chunks of wood and chewing it into splinters.

I pushed Ciara toward the trees and shouted at her, "Find cover! Run for your house!"

As she staggered back toward the trees, I lunged for one of the oars, swung it over my head and brought it crashing down on the nearest cuddly Jaws. Its eyes swiveled in a circle and stars spun over its head as its tongue lolled out. I felt a hand grab my sleeve and I could hear Ciara muttering, "You feckin' eejit!" as she dragged me back toward the trees after her.

Then we were running, dodging trees and jumping over branches.

I said, "Which way?"

She stopped and held up a hand. "Listen!"

I listened. I couldn't hear anything.

She said, "This is bad! This way," and she pushed me to the right. "We have to try to make the road."

Then I heard it. It was like muffled thunder coming up from the ground. We ran. The trees were growing denser and the first autumn leaves were turning to sludge on the moss. I kept slipping and falling and Ciara kept stopping to help me up.

I kept snapping at her, "Keep going! Don't stop!"

And she kept muttering, "Feckin' eejit!"

Then we broke into a clearing and they were on us. Ahead of us was an eight-foot yellow pirate with a parrot on his shoulder. Behind us, a ten-foot yellow troglodyte in a leopard-skin Speedo was wielding a huge club with a nail hammered through it. I bent and picked up a stout branch from the ground and leaned close to Ciara.

I said softly, "I'll draw their attack. You make for the tree

55

cover.

I sprang at the giant yellow pirate. He bellowed an unearthly noise and swung his giant cutlass at me. As I dodged left, it hammered the ground, throwing up splintered branches, stones and grit. I lunged forward, ramming the pointed end of the stick into his knee. The monster bellowed and I rammed it again in a place no man should ever have a pointed stick rammed. His eyes shot out on stalks. Smoke and fire blasted from its ears. He leaned forward and his tongue sprang from his mouth with a jagged speech balloon that said, "OMG! WTF?"

Behind me, I heard a huge crash, but I knew I had to stay focused. So I leaped up, and as I jumped, I stabbed the broken branch into its mouth. That did the trick. As he grabbed the branch with both hands, he dropped the cutlass. It was a huge sword, and I had no idea if I'd even be able to pick it up but I had to try. I grabbed the hilt. It weighed nothing. I swung it over my head, ready to chop the freak's head off. His hair stood on end, his eyes bulged again, his mouth opened to scream and it turned into a giant balloon that made an outrageous farting noise and shot off into the trees.

There was a moment's silence then I heard a cry from behind me. I turned and saw the trog striding away on gigantic yellow legs with Ciara slung over his shoulder. I raised the sword and saw my hand was empty. I screamed, "*Stop!* Come here! It's me you want, you moron!"

I ran. Trog looked back, childishly scared, and began to trot with Ciara bouncing against his back. I was screaming like a crazy man, "Stop, you stupid animal! You'll hurt her! Stop and fight! It's *me* you want!"

But his strides were massive, and as hard as I ran, it was impossible for me to keep up. He reached the top of a rise and vanished over the edge. The last thing I saw before he disappeared was Ciara's head and hair flopping around like a rag doll's. I hit the top of the hill running and fell, rolling and smashing against tree trunks as I went. Small twigs and stones tore at my skin, but as I tumbled, I got glimpses of his huge yellow form bounding down the hill ahead of me through the trees.

God alone knows how I did it, but as I fell, I focused on his mind, and just before I slammed my head into a tree at the bottom of the slope, I got a flash of where he was taking her.

I staggered to my feet. My head was in agony and I felt so sick that I had to vomit right there into the autumn leaves as I ran. It wasn't a pretty sight, but I knew where he was heading, and I reckoned because of his size, he had to take a roundabout route. I could get there quicker dodging through the trees, but I had to be fast. I ran, wiping my mouth with the back of my sleeve like I had all the hounds of Hell on my heels — which was ironic, I guess, because from what I had seen, I was actually on the heels of two of those hounds.

I crested a hill and hurtled straight into a hedgerow but I didn't stop. The twigs and branches tore at my face, my clothes and my skin, but I just plowed on because I knew that Ciara was probably on the other side of those branches. I burst through.

She was.

She was sitting on the back of a twelve hundred CC Harley. There was one huge, hairy Hell's Angel sitting astride that bike and another standing by a similar chopper next to it. We were on a lonely road with no houses and just behind them was a canal. A few Canadian geese looked at us and honked. I glanced around. There was nothing I could use as a sword. I peered at Ciara.

She was pale but mouthed at me, "Go."

I ignored her and turned to the biker who was astride the Harley. I snarled, "Let her go."

He laughed an unpleasant laugh and kicked the bike into life. The engine roared and I ran. I ran for the front wheel. He let out the clutch and hit the gas just as I jumped. I hit him square and my head, which already felt like someone had left an axe lodged in it, smashed into his big, hairy chin. Me, him, the bike and Ciara all went crashing onto the grassy verge of the canal, sliding out of control toward the edge. I somehow grabbed Ciara's wrist with my left hand and dug the fingers of my right deep into the turf as the bike and the Angel slid over the edge with a loud splash.

I heard the other engine roar and turned, staggering to my feet, just in time to see the other Angel accelerating toward me. I was paralyzed—too tired and in too much pain to move. He was less than a second away, with his front wheel lined up, rushing straight at me. There was nothing I could do. It was over. I closed my eyes, gritted my teeth and felt a piercing pain shoot through my legs. Then the ground struck me a shattering blow in the back and I gasped as the air was knocked out of my lungs. Then there was a second loud splash and a gurgling, and a couple of seconds later, I heard Ciara's voice saying, "You are, without a doubt, the biggest fecking gobshite on the face of the earth..." and I opened my eyes just in time to see her lovely face descending toward mine. Our lips touched and all my pain vanished. I closed my eyes and let my arms and my lips do the talking.

Chapter Seven

Neither of us spoke about any of it, which I guess was odd. But the simple fact was that to us, what had happened between us was much more real and important than a couple of shape-shifting, yellow emoticons trying to sink our boat and kill us.

Yeah, I guess on reflection that was pretty strange, but it didn't seem weird to us right then because we had much more amazing stuff on our minds. Like Us, with a big, beautiful, capitalized 'U'. Neither of us could deny, there was now an 'Us'. And we didn't want to.

We walked arm in arm through the woodlands, stopping occasionally to kiss for long, lingering, timeless moments then walked on once more, lost in bliss. Again, as so often happened with Ciara, I couldn't remember afterward what we had talked about. It was like we'd been in a dream that had eventually faded, leaving only the delicious flavor of its meaning but none of the details. I could remember that we talked about how we would find a way to be together, whatever her dad might do or say. We talked about the children we would have and the castle we would live in and the magic we would do. And I almost told her my secret, but I knew there was something I had to do before that. I had to protect my princess.

And I knew, with a stab of fear and pain right through my heart, that if I could not protect her and keep her safe, then I would have to leave her and forget her, because I knew without a shadow of a doubt that those two freaks, those two shape-shifting weirdoes, had come for me. I meant to find out why and do something about it—permanently.

I left her at the fence to her garden where the lawn swept down to the Thames—called the Isis at Oxford—and we kissed in the shade of the trees for a few delicious eternities. Then we finally let each other go and I watched her run like a dancing ray of sunlight across the lawn toward the house.

I made my way back through the town at a very determined pace. Nobody seemed to notice the scruffy kid with the torn clothes and the scratches and grazes all over his face and body. I guess the English have pretty much seen it all, especially in Oxford. And when I checked out some of the undergraduates sloping around the town, I figured they looked worse than I did. Books would do that to you if you weren't careful. I firmly pushed all thoughts of how her eyes were like the green ocean and her hair spun sunlight out of my mind and focused on Gorm and how I was going to tear him limb from limb and eat his heart if he didn't tell me what the hell was going on.

It was just after lunchtime when I got home, and I was pretty sure I had a good two or three hours before Rosie and Dad got back. I marched through the house and out into the garden, straight to the arbor and said very firmly, "Gorm!"

Up on the roof of the shed, a blackbird cocked its head at me, like it thought I was a goldfinch short of a charm. Maybe it was right. All the way here I'd just assumed all I had to do was summon Gorm and have it out with him. It hadn't crossed my mind to wonder how you actually went about summoning a three-thousand-year-old gnome from a parallel universe. I thought about making a pentagram on the grass, but I had no idea how you went about doing that, either. Then it dawned on me that the other night when he'd appeared for the first time, there had been no rituals or pentacles or sacrificial vestal virgins or any of that crap.

I raised my voice and said, "Gorm! I need to talk to you!"

The blackbird tilted its head the other way and sang something complicated into the afternoon air. I tried to remember what I'd done that evening. It had been dusk.

Maybe it needed to be dusk. But if that were the case, how come those two shape-shifting crazies had appeared? There was no doubt in my mind that they had come from the same place as Gorm—and me, for that matter. I paused and thought. I remembered I had been smelling the roses…

I had been smelling the roses, listening to the blackbird and wishing it was a nightingale, because I had just met Ciara and I was head over heels for her. All I wanted was to think about her. I smiled. The blackbird began to sing. I remembered Ciara's kiss on the banks of the canal. A big, idiot grin spread all over my face and I began to hear a very distinctive crackling sound.

Gorm—as ugly as Godzilla on steroids, sitting on the garden bench chewing on half of something that not so long ago had been gamboling in a field, eating clover. He belched and several roses that were in the way withered. He wiped his mouth with the back of an arm that was bigger than most tree-trunks and sighed.

"I was just having breakfast. What is it you want?"

"What do I *want*? I want to know what the *hell* is going on!"

"Am I not just after telling you? I was having me breakfast and the next thing…"

"Gorm! I have just spent the whole damned afternoon fighting off two giant yellow flying emoticons who were trying to drown me, cut me in half with a cutlass and crush me with Harley-Davidsons. I don't give a damn if you were having breakfast!"

He grinned. "Was it the shape-shifting leprechauns, then? Have they been here? Did you give a good account of yourself?"

"Leprechauns? Didn't I just tell you they were giant yellow emoticons?"

"And didn't *I* tell *you* that they were *shape-shifting* leprechauns?" He frowned at me. "You wouldn't have some ale there, would you, lad? No, I seem to remember you never have ale. You know, if you're going to summon me, you might have the courtesy of laying in a bit of ale. A couple of gallons is all I'm saying. Not a vast amount."

I could feel the anger building inside me. "Didn't you tell me? Didn't *you* tell *me*? No, Gorm! No, you did *not* tell me anything about *shape-shifting leprechauns!*"

"Oh—"

"Oh? *Oh?*"

"Did I not? Well, you know, I do sometimes forget things. I'm not as young as I was. I *am* three thousand years old, which is a goodly age, even for a gnome."

"Gorm, they could have killed me! And what is worse, they could have killed Ciara!"

He made an 'oops!' face.

I threw my hands in the air and said, "Who are these guys, Gorm? Why were they trying to kill me?"

He gave an indulgent laugh. "Well now, let's not get carried away. I don't think they was actually trying to *kill* yiz. They was just a little high-spirited. You know what leprechauns are like, after all."

"No…"

"No, well…they get a little excited with all the fun and stuff. But there is…" He screwed up his eyes and scratched his head. "There is something…and I do think perhaps maybe I have been a little, as you might say, bad—"

"Gorm?"

"Yes! Yes! I'm trying to remember. A little ale to lubricate the old brain cells would not go amiss."

"There is no ale, Gorm. You need to tell me who these two guys are and why they were attacking me!"

He nodded. "You're right there!"

"I'm right?"

He raised his eyebrows high on his forehead and gave a wise laugh. "Oooh, yah!" He nodded again. "You're right there, so y'arre!"

"Then *tell me*, Gorm!"

"Well, you remember I told you, you had no *quest* or anything like that, of that sort?"

My skin went cold and prickly. "Yes, I do…"

"Well, I may have been wrong. There may have been *some kind* of a quest…after all…"

I was getting desperate. "What kind of quest, Gorm? C'mon, man. This is important."

He gave that complacent chuckle again and shook his head with a daft smile on his big, ugly face. "The old brain, y'know. T'isn't what it was…" Then suddenly he said, "I know…" and raised a finger. "I know. You have to protect somebody."

I stepped toward him. My franticness turning suddenly to excitement. "Protect *who*?"

His face sank. "Jaysus, isn't that the question? An old man, maybe… It's hard to say exactly."

"Why do I have to protect him? Who from?"

"Excellent questions, to be sure…"

"*Gorm!* You are *so* infuriating!"

"And haven't I been told *that* before? Not least by your own sainted mother!"

"*Gorm!*"

A voice at my shoulder said, "Jake…" I turned and Sebastian was standing there with two six-packs of English beer. He held them out to me. "I found these in your kitchen. They might do the trick."

I stared at him. I wondered where he had come from, took the six-packs and turned to Gorm, who was goggling at the beer with a big, stupid leer on his face.

"I think your friend might be right at that," he said.

I handed them over and he tipped the bottles down his throat whole, without opening them. He chewed, crunched, swallowed then belched — and a couple more roses withered on the bush.

Sebastian stepped forward and spoke. "Gorm, you said that Jake might have a quest. Then you said that quest might be to protect somebody."

Gorm scowled. "I have no feckin' call talking to the likes of you, you wee human pipsqueak. I should be eatin' you raw and grinding up your bones, so I should!"

Sebastian pulled himself erect and, with awesome dignity, said, "It is I, my friend, who brought you the ale. You owe me. And if you wish to drink good English ale in the future, you will treat me with due respect. Do we understand each other?"

Gorm curled his lip. "All right, all right…let me think."

I went to speak but Sebastian interrupted me. "The thing is, Gorm — and you must know this — a quest is a search. So, what should Jake be seeking while he is protecting this old man?"

Gorm stared at Sebastian so long without saying anything that I began to think he'd passed out or dropped dead or something. But finally, he sighed and shook his head. "It's no use, lads. All I can remember is this. Them two feckin' shape-shifting leprechauns are out to cause mischief. They're not in it alone, either. They're too feckin' stupid to do anything on their own. But they are being used by… Let me try to remember… I think, right? I *think* it was Aren."

I said, "Aren?"

"That's right."

"What can you tell us about this Aren?"

"Feck all, Jake. I don't know feck all about him, except that he wants to kidnap an old man — or an elderly man — and it is an important part of your quest to stop him from doing that."

I threw my hands to my forehead and squeezed my eyes shut. "So, let me see if I have this straight. It is your job to inform me about all this sh— All this stuff, right?"

"Right."

"And you are telling me that I have a quest, but you can't remember what it is."

"Right."

"Part of that quest might be to protect an old man from being kidnapped by shape-shifting leprechauns."

"Right."

"But it might not be…"

"Almost certainly is."

"You don't know who this man is."

"Right."

"Or when or why they want to kidnap him."

At this, his face brightened. "Oh, now I can tell yiz a bit about that. It has something to do with all the feckin' mess *his* lot" — he nodded his head toward Sebastian — "are making with the environment. See, we share this planet with them, and before long, it'll be too feckin' hot to live on. So, this feller they're going to snatch has something to do with that. And as to when? Well, isn't it this comin' week? How's that?" He beamed at me, real pleased with himself.

"*This* week?"

"On the Friday, I do believe."

"How the hell am I supposed to help him if I don't even know who he is? On *Friday?*"

He gave a huge belch that made his lips tremble like sea anemones, and he was gone.

We stood in stunned silence for a long while. Eventually Sebastian said, "How could I possibly have believed you? I've seen it with my own eyes and I still don't believe it."

I looked at him and he was shaking his head.

"I'm sorry, Jake."

I put my hand on his shoulder. "Don't worry, buddy. I shouldn't have gone trampling all over your feelings. I had only found out the day before. This Gorm came to me and zap! I was pretty much reeling, and I guess I needed to tell somebody. More to the point, I needed somebody to believe me."

We stood like that a bit then he said, "I get that, Jake. I won't doubt you again." Then he patted my back and said, "Come on, old fellow. Let's go inside. We have a lot of thinking to do. This is the riddle to end all riddles!"

Chapter Eight

We sat at the big table in the kitchen and I made coffee. The light was turning grainy outside, and the blackbird had come back to sing its long, intricate song from the chimney pot.

Sebastian said, "When are you expecting your parents back?"

I looked at the clock over the cooker and said, "Maybe an hour. Maybe a bit more."

He sighed. "I think you should tell me everything from the start. There has to be a clue in there somewhere as to what this quest is and who the old man is."

I nodded. "Okay, and thanks, Sebastian. I appreciate not having to do this alone."

He smiled. "It's what friends are for, old chap. You'd do the same for me."

It wasn't a question, and he was right. I said, "Yeah. I would."

So I told him, from the start, everything that had happened since we'd arrived in Oxford. He sat back and closed his eyes, as though he'd fallen into a deep sleep, but I knew he was using the old Sherlock Holmes technique of totally relaxing his body so that his mind could absorb everything. I finally came to the point where he'd turned up that afternoon, and I shrugged and said, "And you know the rest."

He remained with his eyes closed for another minute then opened them slowly.

"Go back in your mind, Jake, to the time Gorm first appeared to you. Just relax and remember, what were you doing and thinking?"

I sat back and it was my turn to close my eyes. "I'd just gotten back from school. Dad and Rosie were at a drinks party at the dean's. I went out into the back garden."

"What made you do that, Jake?"

I smiled. "I wanted to think about Ciara. I remember I was smelling the flowers and listening to the blackbird and was thinking I wished it was a lark...or a nightingale." I was silent for a minute. Then I said, "You can stop smirking. It was a momentary thing. I'm not a sissy."

He seemed not to hear me. He said, "Now, focus on the moment just before Gorm appeared to you."

"I was standing by the pond. The blackbird was on the chimney. I was thinking about Ciara's eyes and how incredibly green they are. Then the air began to shimmer..."

I talked on for a bit then Sebastian's voice gently interrupted me. "That's very good, Jake. Now, I want you to come forward in time to this afternoon, and I want you to go back into the garden to a few moments before Gorm appeared."

"I was pretty mad. I came through the house with one thought on my mind. I was going to call up Gorm and make him explain what the hell was going on."

"How did you do that?"

I paused. "I couldn't. I called him, but he wouldn't come."

"So, what did you do, Jake?"

"I don't know. I started to remember the first time he appeared. I had been thinking about Ciara and how green her eyes were—"

"And when you started thinking about her?"

"The air changed to a shimmering green."

"Okay, Jake, just take a nice, deep breath, wiggle your fingers and your toes, and when you're ready, open your eyes."

I did those things and stared at him. "Did you hypnotize me?"

"I relaxed you quite deeply with my voice. Do you see the

importance of what you remembered?"

I sat forward. "Ciara."

He nodded. "He appears when you stand by the arbor and think about Ciara."

"Why?"

"We may not have found the answer, old chap, but we seem to have found the question."

"Why?"

He shook his head. "'Why' is the open question to end all open questions. Never ask 'why?' There is no answer to 'why?' The question is 'what?' What is it about Ciara that causes this portal—or whatever it is—to open when you think about her in that particular place?"

I stared at him, shook my head, shrugged and spread my hands. I think I conveyed that I had no idea.

He smiled. "Well, no point thinking about what we *don't* know. So what *do* we know? We can say that there must be some special connection between the two of you. What quantum physicists would call a 'quantum entanglement'."

I smiled. "I like that."

"I thought you might. We have no idea how parallel universes work, but a constant in quantum physics and relativity is the effect of consciousness on reality. So, when you think of her—"

"It affects the reality field!"

He smiled. "If you like. Think of this, also, Jake. When the two shape-shifting leprechauns struck—"

"I was with her."

He nodded. "Indeed, you were. I think you'll find that she is integral to this whole thing."

I frowned. "But why?"

"That's impossible to answer and impossible to find out. 'How', on the other hand, might be easier. Think about it, Jake. What do you know about her?"

I thought. "Not a lot."

"Well, as I say, not much point thinking about what you don't know. But what *do* you know?"

I stood up and started pacing, the way they do in movies. It actually does help you think. I said, "I know she's an only child, and I know she lives alone with her dad."

"Rather like you."

I glanced at him. "Yeah…" I carried on. "Her dad is super-protective and keeps a real tight hold on her. It was almost impossible to meet up today, but she swung it. And she said that because of her dad, it was hard for her to have friends, much less…" I made a 'you know what I mean' gesture with my hand.

He said, "Go out with anybody."

I nodded. "Yeah, that."

"What happened to her mother?"

"I don't know. But I do know her dad is a big shot in politics. Michael Fionn. He's a—"

"He's the guy."

"What?"

"He's the *guy*. He's the man who's going to get kidnapped by this Aren, and it's up to you to protect him—hence the link with Ciara, his daughter."

"How the hell am I going to do that…by next Friday? That's less than a week! And anyway, Sebastian, how can you be sure? Who would want to kidnap—?"

"The chief consultant to the EU on environmental issues? Do you read the news?"

I sat down, feeling a bit sheepish. "Well, not really, no."

"Well, let me suggest that in the future you take a little more interest in the world you live in, Mr. Norgard. Michael Fionn has always been the ultimate man in gray, working behind the scenes while the big personalities get all the limelight. But he is a real mover and shaker. He makes things happen. He is very powerful and *very* influential."

I made a face and while I wondered what the hell I was getting into with Ciara, I asked, "Okay, but how does that make him a target for kidnapping by shape-shifting leprechauns?"

"He has recently sprang into the public eye because he

is due to address the European Commission next week on whether they should sanction drilling for oil in the Arctic Circle. Huge oil reserves have been found there, but when everybody is talking about phasing out fossil fuels and saving polar bears, drilling for oil in the Arctic seems a tad controversial. There is a very powerful lobby saying the EU should put that money into green research for sustainable energy. But there are also vested interests that stand to make billions if the drilling goes ahead."

I nodded. Something was making sense but I wasn't sure what it was. I said, "And what does Michael Fionn say?"

"Precisely. He is playing it very close to his chest, but the word is that he is going to advise they go ahead and drill. It's odd. For many years, he was an advocate behind the scenes for a greener world, but lately he seems to have been drifting the other way."

I screwed up my face and scratched my head, seeing Sebastian suddenly in a different light. "How do you know all this?"

He laughed. "I pay attention, my dear chap! The holy trinity—attention, concentration, observation. And another thing keeps leaping out at me."

I frowned. "What?"

"The color green. Green eyes, green sea, the Emerald Isle, green issues…"

"Holy sh—!"

I stood.

Sebastian said, "What is it?"

I turned to face him. "It's not her dad."

"What do you mean?"

"It's not her dad! It's *her!*"

"I'm not following you."

"We need to find out who Aren is, because he has a vested interest in the advice Michael Fionn gives the EU Commission. He probably stands to make millions, even billions, on the outcome. So, he is going to kidnap Ciara to put pressure on her dad to give the advice *he* wants him to give!" We stared at each other for a long moment. I shook my head. "He hasn't been drifting. He is as green as he has ever been, but he is being threatened and pressured, and that is why he has become so protective of his daughter. *That* is why she knows she can't have friends or—"

"A boyfriend."

I nodded. "Yes, that."

He leaned back in his chair, watching me. "So, what on earth are you going to do?"

I thought about it but not for very long. "I have to talk to Ciara. If I can't get to her tomorrow, then Monday, come what may. I have to get her alone and tell her everything. And whatever happens, on Friday I have to be with her the whole time."

"Good luck with that, old chum. You have your work cut out for you. What about Thursday night after midnight? And what about Friday night?"

I set my jaw. "I'll sleep in the grounds of the house if I have to."

He smiled. "I very much fear you'll have to. I can't see old man Fionn inviting you into his daughter's bedroom. Can you?"

I had to admit I couldn't.

Dad and Rosie came in shortly after that and Sebastian was as easy and charming as though they had been friends forever. He had the weird ability to behave with people twice his age as though he *were* twice his own age. Though I had the uncomfortable feeling when he spoke to Rosie that they were, actually, only a few years apart.

She invited him to stay for tea and we sat on the terrace within sight of the pond, the weeping willow and the arbor. As she offered him a salmon and cucumber sandwich, she said, "Pendrake, is that the Cornish Pendrakes?"

He twitched an eyebrow, but that was as close as he came to showing surprise. "Yes, as far as I know, there are only us and the Devonshire Pendrakes, but we don't talk about them."

It was obviously an inside joke because only he and Rosie laughed.

Dad said, "Why's that?"

He was smiling when he answered. "They supported Cromwell in the Civil War. The Cornish Pendrakes, the oldest branch of the family, supported the Crown."

Dad smiled and shook his head, like he'd never understand the Brits. "You make it sound like yesterday. Wasn't that 1642?"

Rosie laughed. "That *is* yesterday!"

Dad rolled his eyes at me and I smiled.

Rosie turned back to Sebastian. "I believe the Pendrakes are one of the oldest families in England, aren't they?"

He was looking at her a bit fixedly, like he was wondering why she was asking him all this. He said, "There are references to a Celtic Chieftain called Pendrake in Saxon documents going back about fifteen hundred years."

She smiled as she sipped her tea. There was something oddly mischievous about her eyes. "The mighty Uther Pendrake, whose clan were said to have come from Ireland in the dawn of time. I knew your grandfather."

Now, he looked surprised. "Really? But surely…"

She stood. "Oh, there's the kettle. Excuse me."

Sebastian glanced at me. Dad was lost in a sandwich. The blackbird went crazy for a minute. Sebastian said, "And I really ought to be getting back. Mr. Norgard, a pleasure to meet you. See you again, no doubt." And to me, "Jake, see me out, will you?"

We bumped into Rosie on the way to the door and they said brief farewells. At the door, I said to Sebastian, "What the hell was that all about?"

He smiled urbanely and dismissed it. "The English, old chap. We're obsessed with our own language and our ancestry. Very unseemly. Let's try to meet up tomorrow and discuss this business with Ciara. There has to be a more sensible solution than camping out in the old man's garden."

I watched him walk down the drive and wondered how much weirder things could become.

Chapter Nine

Sebastian and I met in town on Sunday and had coffee. We talked, but we talked in circles and came to no conclusion about the best way to proceed except that on Monday I had to talk to Ciara. I thought I should come clean and tell her everything about myself, but Sebastian thought I was crazy. He said Ciara would think the same, to the power of a hundred, and I would just send her running for the hills. I didn't agree. In my gut and in my bones—and in every other visceral part of me—I knew she would be cool with it. But even so, the risk was too high. I had to tell her, but I had to tell her *after* Friday. I couldn't risk her avoiding me before Friday. *No way.*

As it was, it made no difference, because she wasn't there on Monday morning. And to complicate matters, as I was climbing out of Rosie's car, I got a Whatsapp from my teacher, Mrs. Applebotham—pronounced 'apple-bottom', not kidding—saying that I should go straight to the Mooting and Debating Chamber to meet Mr. Singh, join the debating team and receive my first assignment. I cursed in ways that would make Mrs. Applebotham's perm curl and wasted five minutes waiting for Sebastian by the lockers.

As he approached, I said, "Have you seen Ciara?"

He shook his head. "No."

I told him about the Whatsapp and asked him to keep an eye out for her and tell her it was urgent that I see her, wherever and whenever she said—but soon. He said he would and told me where the Mooting and Debating Chamber was. As I was making my way there, I was thinking sourly that it should be the Venerable Mooting and Debating Chamber, and when I got there, I saw a brass plaque outside the ancient oak door that said, *This Venerable Mooting and Debating Chamber was endowed to the school by the Right Honorable Aelfen Nixon in the year of Our Lord 1999.*

I pushed through the door. It wasn't huge, but it was magnificent. The ceiling was gabled and supported by huge oak beams that you just knew were at least five hundred years old. The walls, like most of the school, were oak-paneled. There was a stage at the end of the hall with a lectern on it and rows of benches facing it that I gathered were the public gallery. There was room for maybe two-hundred people.

Sitting at a small table on the stage were four people. There was the headmaster, Mr. Clarendon, the English master, Mr. Singh, who took the debating group, Brutus and a guy I didn't know. They all watched me in silence as I walked down the long aisle between the benches with my steps echoing in the excellent acoustics of the hall. As I reached the stage, Mr. Clarendon said, "Mr. Norgard, good of you to join us." He included Mr. Singh, Brutus and the other guy in a sweeping gesture and said, "You know Mr. Singh and Muller, of course, but Mr. Nixon is new to us, though his family have been patrons of the school for many, many years."

Nixon stood with a kind of languid grace and reached out his hand. "I'm Dicky. I hear good things about your swordplay. We'll have to have a bash sometime."

I shook his hand. It was firm and strong. "Sure. Whenever."

I sat and the headmaster eyed me from under bushy eyebrows. "Mr. Norgard, I have decided to throw you in at the deep end to see whether you will sink or swim. You may view this as a disaster or as an opportunity. I am curious to see which view you take."

He paused and was obviously waiting for an answer, so I said, "I'll certainly view it as an opportunity, sir."

"Glad to hear it. Now, the last couple of weeks have not been uneventful at the Anglo-American, and though we have an excellent record in debating and mooting and many of our best debaters have gone on to excel at the university, our two leading stars this year have both been struck down in the last two weeks in a bizarre outbreak of heinous synchronicity. However, they had performed exceptionally well in inter-school and inter-county debates and have been selected for the national semi-finals. Their teams were the Oxford Owls and Hern." He frowned, I blinked and he went on. "Now, Mr. Nixon here has an outstanding record in debating. He was undefeated at St. Andrews, north of the border, and at St. George's in Paris, from where he comes to us. I am told by his masters at those schools that his oratory is unrivalled and his logic quite crushing in debate. So, I am entrusting him with Hern, and he has agreed to step into the breach, as it were. And to you, Mr. Norgard, I am entrusting the Oxford Owls."

I was astonished and I let my face tell him so. "But, sir, I have never debated in my life!"

"Which is why I am entrusting Hern to Mr. Nixon. My instinct tells me you will flower under pressure, Mr. Norgard. But should my instinct have led me astray, I shall have, as you say on your side of the Atlantic, covered my bases."

"How long have I got to prepare, sir?"

He glanced at his watch and said, "About one hundred and five hours. The debate will be here on Friday evening at six p.m. sharp. I shall expect you here at five. Whoever wins goes through to the finals representing the school."

I half-rose from my chair. "*Friday?* But I can't! Friday is impossible. You need to find somebody else."

His eyes were a couple of degrees colder than the Antarctic ice sheet. "I trust this will *not* be a problem, Mr. Norgard. I have discussed it already with your father and he *fully* understands the importance of the matter. And, may I add that in view of recent events, I shall be expecting great things from you. You have a lot riding on this."

He stood and left.

Mr. Singh was watching me curiously. He spoke suddenly. "Mr. Muller is Mr. Nixon's second. He will assist him in his research and preparation, and, if Mr. Nixon so wishes, he may take part in the debate itself. That is a matter for them."

Brutus was smirking at me like he thought he'd somehow got one over on me.

Singh went on, "You will need to find a second of your own. You have very little time to prepare, and the good reputation of the school rests on your performance, so, Mr. Norgard, I am prepared to give you some latitude in your English schoolwork and homework over the next week."

I was shaking my head, and as I was doing it, I could see Brutus grinning from ear to ear. Dicky was watching me with interest and a kind of mild, superior smile. I ignored them and turned to Singh. "Sir, Mr. Singh, you don't you understand. Any other day but Friday... It is crucial."

"Does somebody's life depend on it, Mr. Norgard?"

I drew breath then hesitated. "Maybe?"

"Whose...and what are the exact circumstances?"

I flopped back in my chair. It was useless.

"I thought not. The subject of the debate is 'Man Has the Right and the Duty to Exploit the Planet's Fossil Fuel Resources'. Hern, you will be defending that statement, and Oxford Owls, you will be arguing against it. If you need help or guidance, you know where to find me."

With that, he slipped us two sheets of instructions, rose and left.

Brutus Muller was leering at me. "So, Norgard, looks like we meet again, huh?"

Dicky didn't even look at him. He just said, "Shut up, Muller." To me, he said, "Catch you in the fencing room this afternoon." And he and Brutus left.

I squinted as I watched them file out. Brutus was carrying Dicky's books.

The rest of the morning passed in a kind of surreal fog. I kept thinking I was going to wake up and everything would have been a wild dream. Whenever I thought about it, it just seemed too absurd to be real, but then I touched my scratches and bruises and I knew it had been *very* real. Besides, Sebastian had been there. He had seen it. Ciara had been there and had almost been killed. It had been real all right, and Ciara was going to be kidnapped and held for ransom if I didn't do something to stop it. But instead of doing something to stop it, I had to prepare for a *damn* debate, because if I didn't win that *damn* debate—or at least make a *damn* good try—I would probably be expelled from the school to the eternal shame and, worse, disappointment of my father.

For less than a second I thought about coming clean with Dad, but I dismissed the idea out of hand. I could just see myself. "Dad, I can't prepare for this debate because, you see, I'm an elf and I have to use my superpowers to rescue Michael Fionn's daughter from shape-shifting leprechauns…"

And by the time I'd run thorough this thought process for the hundredth time, I realized I had absorbed exactly nothing of the class I was in. *Top grades comin' right up, Dad.*

At lunchtime, I met up with Sebastian and we swapped notes—not that there was much to swap. I told him about the debate and Dicky, and he told me he hadn't seen Ciara anywhere. Somebody had said that her dad had phoned her in sick, but nobody was really sure.

At three p.m. I went up to the fencing room and found Dicky there with Brutus. Brutus had his usual smirk that spoke volumes about the level of his neural and synaptic activity. But Dicky was next to him, strapping on his suit, and there was nothing stupid about his face when he smiled at me. There was nothing particularly friendly about it, either.

"Norgard! Good to see you. I've been looking forward to crossing steel with you. I understand you're quite good."

I dropped my bag and unzipped it. The last thing I felt like right then was swashbuckling banter with this bozo. I said, "Sure. Let's do it."

I suited up and we stood *en guard*. His lunge took me by surprise. It was fast, real fast, and I barely parried in time. But I did, then flipped his blade and launched a blistering attack on him. I must have put all the day's frustration into it because he retreated like an express train in reverse, but he parried every single attack. I was momentarily stunned.

We paused to eye each other then we both attacked simultaneously, at the speed of light. Brutus was goggling at us. I don't think he had ever seen anything like it. There were sparks leaping from our blades. It was too fast for any eye to follow and we fought purely by feeling. Not a single thrust got through on either side, and after five minutes, we both stood panting and staring at each other. I felt grudging admiration for him. I was invincible, and he couldn't beat me, but *damn!* I couldn't beat him, either.

He threw his epée on the floor and said, "Sabers!" He turned to Brutus. "Muller! My saber."

Fortunately, my look of astonishment was masked by my helmet as Brutus scrambled to his feet and pulled Dicky's saber from his bag. This guy, Dicky, must pull some serious weight to have Brutus running around as his toady. I walked over and got my saber. We took up our positions again.

I let him attack first and he came at me with a slash to the head. I easily thrust his blade aside and lunged at his chest. I was pretty sure the point would go home, but suddenly my blade was sliding past him, I was half off-balance and his blade was slashing at my side. I rectified with a nanosecond to spare and blocked the slash as I overbalanced. I heard him grunt and he backed away. What he didn't expect was me to attack while still off-balance. I dropped to my haunches and thrust a devastating lunge up under his guard as he retreated. It was game over and another victory to the invincible Jake — only it wasn't. His reflexes were practically superhuman. He blocked me and I avoided having my helmet knocked off by half a hair's breadth.

I retreated. We were both taking gasping breaths. I

focused. There was nothing else in the world. I was going to take this arrogant SOB down. *Now!* I roared as I charged him. I think my blade crossed the light barrier. The sound of steel on steel echoed off the walls. He retreated, turned my attack against me and charged me down so I was galloping backward toward the end of the mat. But I flipped his blade and exposed his chest so he was charging into my blade and, for a flea's heartbeat, I knew I had him. I yelled as my blade skimmed past his vest and before I knew what I was doing, I was blocking a savage slash at my neck.

We retreated again. He threw his saber down with a crash and yelled, "Katanas!"

I said, "I have no katana."

"I have two." He pulled off his helmet, strode to his bag and pulled out two beautiful Japanese samurai swords. He threw one to me. I drew and examined the blade. It was exquisite, but it was not modified for competition. One single slice from one of these babies could take your head off. This guy was crazy. I drew breath to tell him to go to hell, but instead I threw off my own helmet and heard myself saying, "Okay, let's do this."

We ignored the mat. We both knew there were no rules anymore. We fell on each other in a battle to the death. We fought with no restraint. Every blow was a death blow and carried deadly intent. We were fighting for our lives, but above all, we were fighting to win, and to hell with the consequences. His speed and skill were astonishing. No normal person could have withstood the devastating power of his attacks. Yet I had him retreating, sweating and struggling to resist the hail of blows I rained down on him. It was a miracle we didn't die there.

We staggered away from each other, gasping for breath. He was smiling and shaking his head. "How?"

Before I could answer, he raised his blade for me to look at. I checked my own. They were chipped and dented like pieces of driftwood.

He stared at me and he said, "Viking broadswords. Let's

finish this."

He stripped off his fencing suit down to his jeans and a bare chest. I did the same. He threw me a stunningly crafted Viking battle sword and we charged each other without preamble. Things got brutal. I don't know how long it went on, but I was possessed by a berserker rage and I know he was, too. If anybody had tried to stop us right then, it would have gone badly for them. Any one of the blows we rained down on each other would have severed a limb or split our skulls down the middle. We didn't care. I remember swinging two terrible blows right to left and back again that would have cut him in half if they had connected. He jumped back and sprang onto the table that ran along the back wall. From there, he laid two massive blows down at my head. I blocked both and swung at his legs. He leaped and thrust down at my neck. I deflected the blow and rammed my right forearm into his legs. He came crashing down on his back. Without thinking, I rammed the blade down, double-handed and plunged it through the table up to the hilt, an inch from where he had been lying just before.

I was disarmed, but his sword was lying on the floor at my feet. He had sprung to his haunches to avoid my deathblow and our faces were inches away from each other. We were breathing hard, staring into each other's eyes.

He said, "I think I have seen all I need to see, Norgard, and so have you. Are you as good with a bow?"

I nodded. He dropped down from the table. He spoke to Brutus without looking at him. "Collect my weapons, Muller."

In silence, I watched him dress while Brutus scurried around gathering up his swords and his kit, packing them into his bag. Finally, while he was buttoning his shirt, he spoke.

"You are the best swordsman I have ever met." Then he turned toward me. "And I have fought the best." He repeated it, like he was making a point. "The best. And you are better than them."

I shrugged. "I guess I had a lucky day."

His face told me what he thought of that. He raised a hand and pointed at me. "Let's be friends, Norgard. People like us should be friends. We should not be enemies."

When he'd gotten to the door and Brutus was about to open it for him, I said, "Who said anything about enemies?"

He stopped and turned back.

I added, "Apart from you."

He shook his head. "Nobody, apart from me. Don't cross me, Norgard. Let's be friends."

I said, "It's a debate. Aren't you getting a little serious?"

He smiled. "A debate? Friday is a lot more than a debate. You should know that."

Then he left.

I dressed and gathered my stuff, wondering what the hell had happened just then and what the hell had happened to me. I am not Erik Blacktooth. I am a nice, well-educated, American kid, but I had been about to cut this guy in half with a Viking broadsword—or rend him asunder or cleave him in twain.

I went back down the stairs, thinking absently that I could really use a flagon of ale. You do, after a battle to the death with broadswords.

I found Sebastian waiting for me on the steps outside the school. He looked me over and said, "What on earth have you been up to now?"

I smiled. "Does it show?"

"Rather, old chap." He stood and we fell in step toward the gates. "I've asked about. Nobody seems to know anything about Ciara. Short of asking some of her tutors, I don't know what we can do."

I shook my head. "No, that would arouse too much curiosity. She'll probably be in tomorrow. We still have four days. If she isn't here, then we can think again."

I left him at the gates and walked home in a state of deep confusion.

Chapter Ten

But Ciara didn't turn up Tuesday – or Wednesday, either. While I waited for her to show, I spent long hours working on the debate. By which I mean that I spent long hours staring at the piece of paper Mr. Singh had given me while thinking about Ciara and wondering where she was. At one point, about two a.m. on Wednesday morning in a fit of furious motivation, I wrote the words *Ladies and Gentlemen*. Then I visualized Ciara's face in the audience, looking up at me. I stood and started pacing the room. At four a.m., I collapsed on the bed and by five I had fallen into a fitful sleep. Two hours later, my alarm went off. I fell out of bed, clawed my way across the carpet to the bathroom, showered then sat for an hour staring at the piece of paper that had *Ladies and Gentlemen* written on it while wondering where the hell Ciara was and if she would show up for school that day. If she didn't, I had a real problem.

But I knew she wouldn't – and I was right.

At eleven I had a tutorial with Mr. Singh to discuss the progress on the debate. The idea was that I would deliver what I had written so far as a piece of oratory, and he would give me advice on content, style and my delivery. When I told him all I had managed to write was *Ladies and Gentlemen*, he sighed, got up from his desk and went to look out of the window. That is never a good sign. When people do that, they are usually about to tell you something you really don't want to hear.

After a moment, he said to the view outside, "Jake, you haven't been here long, but you're a likeable chap and people seem to care about you. Nobody is keen for you to leave under a cloud." He turned and stared at me, giving the words time to sink in. "And I am quite certain you want to make your father proud."

"Yes, sir."

"But, I don't know if you are aware of this. Mr. Muller's father carries a certain amount of weight in this school. He has made a number of generous endowments..."

"I see, yes."

He walked back to his chair and sat. He was trying hard to help me. I could tell that. He went on. "Strictly off the record, Jake, after the recent incident, we need a good reason to keep you on. We need you not only to keep your nose clean, but we also need a good academic performance. We need you to be a positive asset for the school. Debating is the way forward for you. What I am trying to say is that the headmaster is offering you a lifeline with this."

"I know, sir..."

"I would really, very *strongly*, advise you, Jake, to make the most of it."

"Yes, sir."

"Now, please. Go now and prepare your debate. Bring me something we can use."

I went straight to the library and dug out every book, article and essay I could find on the subject of fossil fuels and how their exploitation is devastating vulnerable animals, habitats and humanity itself. I piled them on my desk and stared at them unseeingly for three-quarters of an hour, thinking about how badly I was about to let my dad down.

At lunchtime, I put them all back again, unread, and went in search of Ciara and Sebastian. I found Sebastian waiting for me outside the dining hall.

"Before you ask, no, I haven't seen her and neither has anybody else. She has vanished without so much as a puff of smoke. What's happening with your debate?"

I glanced at him. "What debate?"

We collected our food and found a quiet spot in the far

corner of the hall. We sat and I said, "There's only one thing to do, Sebastian."

He prodded his mashed potatoes resignedly and said, "Oh, God."

"I have no choice. I have to contact her. I *have* to find out where she is. Her life could be in danger."

He put a slice of roast beef in his mouth and ruminated for a while. Finally, he said, "I know. What are you going to do?"

"I'll have to go to her house."

"They'll never let you in, and you'll alert them to the fact that you're after her."

I sighed and rubbed my face. "Okay, so this is the age of communication. She has to be on Facebook, Twitter, Instagram…"

"With *her* father? You're joking! They won't even be in the phonebook."

"What about friends? Girlfriends? Did you ever see her hanging out with anyone?"

He was shaking his head before I'd even finished. "Forget it, Jake. Michael Fionn has decided to isolate his daughter, and there's no way you are going to get to her through any of the normal channels." He realized what he had said too late. He looked at me and I looked at him. He said, "Oh, God, Jake, what are you going to do?"

I pushed my food around my plate for a bit while he watched me. Finally, I said, "If I can't reach her through a normal channel, I'll have to use an abnormal one. I'll have to go there tonight."

"What are you talking about?"

"I'll have to break in."

"Are you insane?"

"I don't think so. What are my options? You said yourself that there's no way I'm going to get to her through any of the normal channels. I haven't got time to mess around, Sebastian."

"Have you any idea what will happen to you if you get

caught? That is burglary in British law! You could go to prison!"

"Okay, fine! So you tell me. What are my other options?"

He flopped back in his chair and shook his head. "I honestly don't know, Jake, but as your friend, I have to warn you against this. I have to. I have a really *bad* feeling about this."

I nodded. "I know…" I spread my hands. "But…"

He sighed and dropped his fork on his plate. "When do you plan to do it?"

I thought for a moment. "I need to prepare a bit. Tomorrow night."

"You want me to help?"

I smiled at him. "Thanks, Sebastian. I appreciate it, but it's best if I go alone."

He nodded. "For God's sake, don't get caught."

* * * *

It was a September moon. The sky was a deep, translucent blue, but a few clouds, like the silhouettes of tall ships backlit by moonlight, sailed quietly on the night. I looked at the clock on my cell. It was five minutes to midnight and the house was dark and silent. I had my rucksack packed and ready by the window. I slipped up the sash and the night air brushed my face, rich with the rich smells of damp grass, the sweet and the musty tang of the fallen leaves of autumn.

I slung the rucksack on my back, slipped out of the window and by using the drainpipe and the ivy that swarmed up the side of the house, I was able to make it more or less silently down to the lawn. A quick sprint got me past the arbor and down to the back fence. Then it was a steady trot cross-country, through fields and hedgerows for half an hour until I came to the woods that abutted Ciara's house on the banks of the Isis.

I lay on my belly, on a bed of damp, pungent leaves

and moss under a giant chestnut tree, trying to pierce the darkness with my eyes and see into the haze of shadows around the house. There was nothing but sleepy stillness. Around me, small things rustled and snuffled through the dead leaves and the undergrowth. Then a spotlight snapped on at the back of the house. By its light, I saw a cat, its shadow stretched and dancing grotesquely across the lawn. It trotted to the back of the house and disappeared. After a minute, the light winked off and silent shadows engulfed the garden again. I waited. No lights came on in the house. Nothing happened.

I got up and vaulted silently over the wooden fence. I stayed crouching on the grass for twenty seconds. Still, nothing happened. So I sprinted across the lawn to the rose bushes that flanked the patio. The spotlight snapped on and I ducked behind the bushes and crawled up to the back wall of the house then along to the kitchen door. There was no cat-flap, but there was no cat, either. I waited, motionless, until the light winked off again.

There was no doubt this guy was going to have an alarm system. The question was what kind? I wondered if the cat belonged to the house and came and went as it pleased. If it did, I could be fairly sure the system did not have a motion sensor. But I could be equally sure that if I tried to force a window or a door, I would trip some kind of an alarm and the cops would be all over me in a matter of minutes. I really hadn't thought this through. *Always think your plans through. Make the long movie.*

I was telling myself this, rather pointlessly, when I heard a gentle meow above my head. I looked up and saw the same cat I'd seen before, sitting on a ledge on the first floor, peering at me in the way cats have that makes you feel somehow stupid. And thinking that gave me a stupid idea. If I could read people's minds, could I read an animal's mind? I focused on the cat, on whether it could get in and out of the house and if so, how?

Nothing happened except that I got a kind of mental white

noise and the cat watched me, seeming vaguely amused. Then it stood with its tail straight up and trotted along the ledge toward a window, where it hunkered down then disappeared. It was impossible to see in the dark, especially with the ledge in the way, but two got you twenty that the sash window was a couple of inches open to let Fluffums squeeze in and out. It was also about ten feet up a sheer wall with no drainpipe and no ivy.

I backed up a few paces. The spotlight snapped on. I sprinted and, as I reached the wall, I leaped. It was just about the right height for me to grab the ledge with my fingertips. I heaved with all my might, scrabbled with my toes and managed to haul myself up until I had my elbows on the ledge. I was right. The window was open three inches — enough to be invisible from below but allow the cat access. I reached out and hooked my left hand inside. With the other, I eased up the sash another couple of feet, enough to allow me through. Then I pulled and I was inside.

It was a bedroom. The only light was the moonlight from outside. I hunkered down on the carpet, very still, thinking and listening to the sounds of the house. Apart from the odd creak of old timber expanding or contracting in the changing temperatures, it was perfectly silent. Something felt very wrong. I kept asking myself why a man who was so paranoid about his daughter's safety would have such lax security in his house. I stood cautiously and moved around the room. My eyes were adjusting to the penumbra and I could just make out a queen-sized bed, a bedside table with a lamp and a wardrobe. It was hard to see colors, but it all looked a bit pink and frilly — not over the top, but pretty girly. It felt like it could be Ciara's room, especially with the window being open for the cat, but there were no photos, no fluffy bears, no personal objects of any type — and above all, there was no Ciara.

I stepped over to the door. It was ajar. I pulled it gently open. It squeaked loudly. I froze. Listened. Nothing. I stepped out onto the landing. The house was as silent as a tomb. In front of me there was a balustrade above a stairwell. To my right, there were two doors and a third in the wall facing me. To my left, there was another door where the wall made a right angle. I crept over to it and took about thirty seconds turning the handle. Then I gave it a quick push so it wouldn't squeak. The room was dark, but I could just recognize the bulk of a large, king-size bed. I listened for breathing or snoring. Nothing. I stepped two steps closer to the bed till I could see it in the faint moonglow from the window. It was empty, and like the other room, the bedside tables had no photos, no books, no glasses—no personal objects of any type, except I noticed a crucifix over the bed. It crossed my mind absently that he was Irish and probably a Catholic.

I stood staring and mentally scratching my head for a while. Then, a little less carefully I made my way to the other bedrooms. They were also empty. In the bathroom, there were the usual soaps and shampoos but no toothpaste and no toothbrushes.

They had moved out.

To where?

I went to the top of the stairs and listened. I knew what I was going to hear. *Nothing.* So, I trotted down and found an open-plan kitchen-breakfast room, a large oak-paneled dining room, a drawing room with a walk-in fireplace the size of a small house and a study that was locked.

It was locked at first, but after I applied some wire from my rucksack to it, it clicked open and I stepped in. The room was very dark. There were heavy curtains drawn across the windows and a strong smell of pipe tobacco. I felt my way to the desk and snapped on the lamp. It cast a pool of amber glow over dark wood and green leather. There was a black leather swivel chair behind the desk and in front of it a Chesterfield sofa and an armchair in a rich, washed green leather. I put my backside on the edge of the desk and stared around the room for a while, letting the things I saw sink in slowly, letting my mind look without me interfering for some clue to where they had gone. There didn't seem to be anything of any particular interest, nothing unusual or out of the ordinary.

If they had left suddenly in the middle of school term, that was something he would have had to organize unexpectedly, and it occurred to me that that was something you would do from your desk — on the phone. I had a flash of an image of my dad making the arrangements to move from Boston to Oxford. I saw him at his desk, the phone in his left hand and jotting down details with a pen in his right hand — on a notepad.

I turned and surveyed the desk. The phone was there in its cradle. There was a notepad with a pen laid across it. There was nothing written on the pad, but I'd seen enough detective movies to know what to do next.

I dropped into the chair and pulled a pencil from his penholder. I rubbed it very gently over the pad, and sure enough, a couple of words began to appear — *St. Mary's* and underneath it, underlined three times, *Little Sodbury*.

St. Mary's. On an impulse, I pulled out my iPhone and googled St Mary's, Little Sodbury. It said it was one of the few Catholic parish churches in England dating back to the Reformation. It was noted for its elaborate gilded carvings, statues and its crypt, which was currently closed to the public because of its state of disrepair. There was a telephone number listed. I leaned over and picked up the phone from the cradle and scrolled down to last number redial.

The last number Michael Fionn had called from that phone was St. Mary's. They were there, absolutely no doubt in my mind. Thirty seconds on Google told me that Little Sodbury was just twenty miles away to the north. That was no distance at all, unless you were on foot. I had my license, but what I didn't have was a car.

I could see in my mind's eye the garage next to the house. It was a large garage. I could also see Ciara being picked up by her dad in a dark-blue, brand-new Jaguar. It was a car that you noticed—the kind of car you wouldn't use if you wanted to keep a low profile and disappear for a while. The kind of car you'd leave in the garage while you rented something anonymous like a VW Polo.

And you would leave the keys where? Somewhere safe? I glanced around the study again, but even as I was looking, I knew that was wrong. His mind was on making his daughter safe, not his car. The key to the Jag would be in a fruit bowl on the kitchen countertop.

I got up and went next door.

It wasn't in a fruit bowl. That's where women leave their car keys. It was on a hook on the corkboard by the door. I stepped out into the night. The automatic door to the garage rumbled loudly in the darkness. My belly was burning and my heart was racing. What I was doing was totally crazy. If Dad had the faintest idea, he'd go insane. I was going to be in so much trouble. I would be expelled from the school. This was theft—theft of a motor vehicle. Grand theft auto. I could be arrested. I was seventeen. I'd be tried as an adult. I could even go to prison. I'd have a criminal record for the rest of my life. If I walked away now, I could pretend nothing had happened, go back home to bed, forget the whole thing and trust that Michael Fionn knew what he was doing and was the right man to protect his daughter. But the minute I climbed in that car and pressed the ignition, there would be no turning back.

The door came to a halt with a crash. I stepped forward and the lights came on automatically. And there it sat, looking at me with hungry eyes, like a big cat ready to pounce. The Jaguar F-Type, gleaming under the buzzing strip lights, three liter supercharged V6 engine, three hundred seventy-four break horsepower of pure grunt, zero to sixty in four point eight neck-breaking seconds, top speed of one hundred seventy miles per hour. *All mine, all mine, all mine.* I muttered, "Come to Papa, baby," and climbed in.

My criminal career had begun. Victory was for the brave. There was no turning back.

Chapter Eleven

I will tell you one thing I learned about driving a Jag with nearly four hundred break horsepower that accelerates from zero to sixty in less than five seconds. You don't ever press your foot down on the accelerator. *Never*. Not unless you have a penchant for getting kicked in the ass by four hundred horses all at the same time. What you do is, you *think* about brushing the gas pedal with the air particles between the sole of your shoe and the pedal then you grip the steering wheel, close your eyes and pray for a painless death.

I put it in gear, let out the clutch, touched the gas — and screamed. This monster lunged out of the garage, hit the gravel spewing stones into the air, gripped the path with its claws and hurled itself toward the gate, making a noise like a starving leviathan trying to eat a pack of crazed lions. I made the mistake of shifting up to second gear and exited the gate sideways, torturing the tires. I changed up to third, put my foot on the gas and began to enjoy myself. Fourth, and I was surfing a giant tsunami on steroids through a narrow funnel of light. The hedgerows were the skeletons of banshees and hags that sprang out of the blackness, reaching at me with gnarled arms and fingers. The huge V6 growled and the wraiths were swept away into the shadowlands behind me.

I got to Little Sodbury in about twelve minutes. The town was dark but for a few melancholy street lamps in the main square, set around the village green. I slowed to a rumbling crawl, looking for the church spire. A fox loped across the common, its shadow eerily stretched and dancing in the dull, amber light. From the hedgerows, small eyes caught my headlamps for an instant and glowed a weird green. Then, like a ghastly shroud rising out of the graveyard, the church tower rose, not tall and pointed but squat and pale with battlements in the Norman style.

I killed the engine and climbed out. The car door slammed loudly in the stillness and the echo of my feet ricocheted off the slumbering shops and houses. I felt certain people must be hearing me and going to their windows to peer out, to see who was violating their peace. I stepped into the graveyard. The trees, tall poplars and massive yews, closed about me. An owl hooted and made the skin crawl on the back of my neck. I scanned the area and saw the great bird spread its wings and take off, silent as a shadow, into the night.

The church tower was an ink stencil against the sky, surrounded by the indistinguishable black shapes of trees and rooftops. I stumbled up the path, listening for any sound that might help me to find Ciara or her dad but hearing only the rustles, whispers and snuffles of small, secret animals in the shadows—not vampires, but hedgehogs, foxes, owls and cats. Yet these sounds seemed merely to whisper across the face of a darkness that lurked beneath them, like an emptiness from which only evil could emerge. I reached the top of the path and came to the vast Norman door set in the bell tower. I pushed at it, but it was locked and as solid as a block of granite. I peered through the keyhole but saw nothing.

The path encircled the church and I guessed it led to the vicarage at the back. Only this wasn't a vicarage, I reminded myself. It was a Catholic church, and that was why her dad had come here to protect his daughter. Something about that troubled me, but at that moment, my mind was too occupied to see exactly what it was. I got to the back and searched along the path, not sure what I was looking for. I really hadn't planned this properly. But how could I? I was making it up as I went along. I had no other choice.

At first, it seemed like everything was dark and still and silent. I sighed with frustration, wondering what the hell to do next. I was about to turn back when something caught the corner of my eye. I froze and scanned the area again. I know there are things you can see with your peripheral vision that you cannot see straight on, so I moved my head around as though I was just about to turn away, trying to capture again what I had glimpsed before. If anyone had spotted me, they would have thought I was out of my mind, but it worked. Just where the church wall bent in to meet the later building of the priest's residence, there was an almost invisible glow of light on the grass.

I sprinted over to it as silently as I could. I had struck the jackpot. At ground level, there was an arched window a foot across and not more than six inches at its highest point. It had three iron bars set in it, and there was light filtering out. I dropped to my belly and peered in. It was hard at first to make out what I was seeing because of the grime on the glass and the angle I was at. But finally, I saw them. There was a middle-aged man in black with a shock of white hair swept back from his face. He was standing and seemed to be talking, though I could hear nothing of what he was saying. There was another man sitting opposite him. He was harder to make out, but he appeared to be about forty-five or fifty, and he was dressed in a tweed jacket and dark pants. I guessed he was Michael Fionn, because Ciara was sitting next to him, staring at her feet with her hands between her knees.

I had found her. That, at least, was something.

Then I became aware of something else. It was a pair of feet in very shiny black shoes. Because of where I was looking from, I couldn't see any more than the feet and two slim legs in black trousers from just below the knees. They were standing at right angles to the guy in black, whom I assumed to be the priest. They were quite still while the priest talked. Ciara's dad appeared worried and Ciara seemed depressed. For some reason, those black feet made me feel really uncomfortable.

Then they moved. They stepped forward and turned toward Ciara and her dad. Now I could see the whole body, but from above and to the side. I could see the top of the head and the silhouette. It was a man. He was also dressed all in black. He was slim and young and athletic, and there was something about him that was familiar. Then he stepped forward and hunkered down just in front of Ciara and took her hands in his. She looked up into his face. I couldn't decipher her expression, but her body language was receptive. My heart skipped and there was a hot pellet in my belly. I knew him. I knew him very well and I knew he was very dangerous.

It was Dicky Nixon.

My mind was suddenly on fire. *What is he doing here? What is he saying to her? Why does she seem to be smiling at him and listening? Can't she see him for what he is?* I was suddenly in a fever. For a fraction of a fraction of a second, I was going to read her mind, but I recoiled from the thought. It would be the ultimate betrayal of our trust, and there would be no coming back from that. But him? I owed him nothing and I knew — like I knew I had bones in my body — that he meant her no good. I fastened my mind on him and focused.

And I was hit by an express train. I was actually knocked back an inch from the window. My head was reeling. I stared down and saw that he was staring straight up at me. His eyes were locked on mine like a vise. He was rising to his feet, moving toward me, and I could feel the steel fingers of his mind reaching inside mine, gripping at me, and I could hear him demanding, "Who are you? Who *are* you?"

I wrenched myself away and rolled. I scrambled to my feet and ran. My head was reeling with questions, but one thing I was absolutely certain about was that my presence there was putting Ciara at risk. I had to go. For her safety — for her life — I had to get out of there. *Now!*

I ran like all the hosts of Hell were on my heels. For all I knew, they were. I skidded around the corner and raced down the path. I vaulted a stone tomb, stumbled and fell. But I was on my feet again and running practically before I'd hit the ground. Something big and black swooped overhead. The trees rustled. I vaulted another stone tomb and skidded to the gate, grabbed the post then skidded around it and I was running across the common toward the Jag.

A voice bellowed, "*Oi!* You! Stop!"

I skidded for the third time, stopped and turned back. It was a cop—what the Brits call a bobby—standing in the middle of the common, staring at me. His face was in shadow under his helmet, under the street lamp. There was no cop car. He was just standing there, looking at me. I thought I heard him say to come over there, but as I went to step toward him, I realized I hadn't heard him speak. I swore—"Shit!"—turned, ran and jumped into the Jag convertible without opening the door. I hit the ignition and was burning rubber, screaming out of there while he was sprinting across the square toward me.

I side-slid into the corner, and as I accelerated away, back toward Oxford, I could see him in my rearview, thumping down the road after me freakishly fast. My heart seemed to be doing two-forty to the minute and my breathing was ragged. I felt sick and my hands were trembling. My mind was in turmoil. I had left Ciara back there with those creatures, but I knew beyond any doubt that if I had stayed, it would have been disastrous for her. It might have cost her her life.

I needed to think—coldly, rationally. I had to *think*!

I was swerving wildly on the road, fighting to control the machine. I looked at the speedometer. I was doing one hundred miles per hour on a winding country road. Something black swooped overhead. I glanced up. The black stencil of a giant bat or an eagle swooped over me and soared up into the night sky, banked and glided across the moon. I inhaled deeply, steadied my breathing, relaxed my arms on the wheel and eased off the gas to pull over. I had to stop the storm in my mind. Stop the chaos. *Still waters. Blue skies. Stillness.* I focused on these. *A still lake. A still lake under a still, blue sky. Stillness.*

What did I know for a fact? I knew that I'd had to leave or it would have cost Ciara her life. *Fact.* I knew I could not leave her there. I had to rescue her. *Fact.* Therefore, inescapable deduction, I had to return, better prepared with foreknowledge and with a plan how to get her out.

I knew that Friday was the day when they were going to go for her. *Fact.* I knew it was already Friday. *Fact.* And I knew that Dicky was there with her, that he was an invincible swordsman and a mind reader. He had to be one of them — or us! *Fact.* So, the inescapable deduction was that they already had her. I could feel the wild storm starting again in my chest and in my brain. I breathed. *Still waters. Still sky.*

Another fact was that I could not do this alone. I needed help. I needed a plan and I needed help to make it and carry it out, and there was only one person I knew I could count on. I checked the clock on the dash. It was two-twenty a.m., and we both had school in the morning. And I had a debate — a debate that would decide whether I stayed at the Anglo-American or was kicked out. A debate for which I hadn't even written the first words.

I buried the thought as soon as it reared its head. That was the least of my worries. Ciara's life was in danger. She had been kidnapped along with her father — whose car I had stolen — and I had supernatural shape-shifters chasing me. I pulled my cell from my pocket, opened Whatsapp and found Sebastian.

U awake?

Twenty seconds later, I got a response.

Of course I'm not awake. It's 2.20 in the morning, you ass!

I need ur help.

At 2.20 in the morning? Go back to sleep, Jake.

I'm not in bed. I'm in Michael Fionn's Jag. I stole it.

He went off line and a few seconds later the phone rang. I put it on speaker.

"Are you out of your tiny, fucking *mind?*"

"I can't explain now, Sebastian. This is huge. It is bigger than we thought. It's a mess. You have to help me. I have no one else to turn to."

"Shut up, Jake. Don't get your bloody knickers in a twist. Of course I'm going to help you. What do you want?"

"I'll pick you up at the corner of your street in ten minutes. We need to talk. And we need to act *tonight.*"

I heard him groan and he hung up. The car and the night felt suddenly desolate, empty and lonely in the immense darkness. Above my head, I saw the black silhouette pass over the moon again — circling, hunting. And as the reality of what was happening hit me, I felt a piercing terror go through my body.

I stared hard at the road, gripped the wheel and started driving.

Chapter Twelve

He was at the corner, as he'd said he would be. He had his rucksack with him and when he climbed into the car, he pulled out a flask of coffee and a couple of cold croissants. I drove to a quiet spot near the river, put up the hood and killed the lights. He passed out coffee and croissants and we sat, dunked and drank in silence for a while.

Finally, he said, licking his fingers, "Well?"

"Sebastian, I really need your help."

He snorted. "You're not wrong on that score, old mucker. You are right up shit creek without a paddle. You've got yourself into a right bloody mess, haven't you?"

"Listen. I went to Ciara's house and broke in."

He stared at me like I was insane. "You broke in?"

"I didn't *break* in, exactly. There was a window open and I slipped in."

"What? Sort of by accident…on a banana skin?"

"Shut up, Sebastian! I had to see where Ciara was, but the house was empty. I scoured the place from top to bottom. Then, in her father's study, I found he'd made arrangements to go to Little Sodbury, to the Catholic church there."

He made a face and nodded. "That makes sense, I suppose. God alone knows what Ciara told him about your jaunt on the boat, but it must have scared him half to death."

"Well, it made sense to me, too. That's why I borrowed his car and went over there. I was hoping to talk to them and persuade him that I had to be with Ciara. I didn't have much hope of that, but it was already Friday and I had to do something, right?"

He rubbed his eyes with his fingertips. "I suppose you

did, Jake. Yes, I suppose so..."

"Well, I found the place locked up, but there was a small window down at ground level and I could see through it into some part of the crypt. They'd fixed it up with chairs and stuff. And they were there — the priest, Michael Fionn and Ciara."

He nodded then frowned. "So, did you speak to them? What happened?"

"I didn't. I couldn't."

"Why?"

"There was somebody else there."

He waited, staring at me. He asked, "Who, Jake?"

I felt a sick twist of anxiety in my gut that I couldn't identify. I said, "Dicky Nixon."

"Dicky Nixon? The new boy?"

I nodded. "He was crouching in front of her, holding her hands. I think she was smiling."

His eyebrows shot up again. "Oh..."

I shook my head. "No. I'll admit that just for a bit I was tempted, but I trust her, Sebastian, like I trust myself. More. But him? I wouldn't trust him as far as I could drop kick him — and that's a long way."

"You're jealous, Jake. You're not objective."

"I tried to read his mind, Sebastian. He detected it and looked straight at me. I felt him reaching inside my mind, trying to find out who I was. His mind is powerful. It held me like a vise and I could hardly break away."

Sebastian rubbed his chin. He seemed worried. But he appeared worried for me, not Ciara. He said, "Jake, I hate to say this, but as you weren't able to protect her, maybe they sent someone else."

My belly burned and I felt my face flush. "No! He is a danger to her, Sebastian. I know it. If I hadn't left there, something would have happened to her. I knew it. I could *sense* it!"

"You're not objective."

"I *know it!*"

He sighed. "Fair enough. I believe you. So, he is one of them...you..."

I nodded. "And I'm pretty sure the shape-shifters work for him. He has some kind of power over people. He can control them. Have you seen what he's done to Brutus?"

He shook his head.

"Well, he has him running around like his lackey. And he had some kind of shape-shifter chasing me when I left."

We were quiet for a while. Then he said, "He has the same powers as you, but he has had more time to practice them—sword fighting, archery and telepathy. Gorm said you might have others he couldn't remember, right?"

"Yeah..."

"Well, mind control and telepathy are very close, aren't they? You are both very eloquent. You have the gift of blarney, as Ciara put it. That's why you're supposed to be debating against each other today. Bit of a coincidence, that, wouldn't you say?"

"What are you saying?"

"If you applied your eloquence to your mind reading, wouldn't you be able to control people? Manipulate their minds? A kind of super NLP?"

"I don't know. Maybe... What are you driving at, Sebastian?"

"Think about his name. What is his name again?"

"Dicky Nixon..."

"What's Dicky short for?"

"Richard..."

"Richard Nixon? Seriously?"

I spread my hands. "It's a bit odd, but maybe his parents—"

He interrupted me. "What are his initials, Jake?"

"His initials? R.N...."

"R.N....Aren. Ring any bells?"

"Shit."

"It gets better. What are your initials?"

"J.N. I don't get it..."

"Jayen? The last phoneme is the same. Maybe it isn't one name. Maybe it's a name and a surname. Ar En and Jay En."

I shook my head. "No... No!"

"Think about it, Jake. You have the same powers, you are involved in the same bloody fiasco and it seems you have the same—or at least related—names, but he remembers and you don't."

I suddenly grabbed him by the scruff of his neck with both fists. There was a wild panic in my belly. "We have to get to her, Sebastian. I have to get back to her. I *know* she is in danger."

He clasped my wrists and stared into my face. "Take it easy. Stay cool. You said you need my help and you do. Keep your head screwed on and stay *cool*, or you are going to fuck up and get everybody killed. Do you read me?"

I relaxed and flopped back in my seat. "Okay...yes."

"We need a plan. And we need to execute it systematically and coolly. Got it?"

I nodded. "Yes." I tried to think but couldn't. I asked, "What plan, Sebastian? Help me..."

"Shut up and I will. As far as I can see, there is only one way of doing this, but it puts a huge risk on you. We have to face this, Jake. It could cost you your life. Are you prepared for that?"

I stared at him. "To save Ciara, yes."

"There are just two of us against at least three of them, and one of us is a mere mortal. That puts huge pressure on you."

I frowned, suddenly realizing what I was asking of him. "It also puts you at risk, Sebastian."

He shrugged and smiled. "That's the thing with life, Jake. None of us gets out alive. Now listen. The best way we can use our resources is this. You are going to have to take on Dicky and the shape-shifters on your own. You are invincible but so is he. So, it should be a stalemate. You understand your purpose is not to beat them—at least not

Dicky. Your aim is to create a stand-off and keep them occupied."

I nodded. "Okay, and meanwhile you slip in and get Ciara and her dad out to the car."

"Exactly, but you'll have to do one more thing. While you are fighting them with your sword, you are also going to have to keep up a sustained attack on Dicky's mind. A constant assault, you understand, so that he has not an ounce of attention to pay to anything else. Only that way can I get past him without his realizing and get Ciara out."

"Holy sh—!"

"It will likely be utterly draining. For all I know, the effort might kill you. I don't know. But as far as I can see, it is the only way we can pull this off. Are you really prepared to do this?"

I stared at him a long while. Finally, I said, "And you? Would you be prepared to risk your life to do this?"

He shrugged. "Got to be done, hasn't it?"

"Then, of course, I am prepared to do it." I clasped his hand in mine. "And I will forever call you my brother."

I think he blushed. English guys don't go for all that stuff. He gripped my hand, made some waffling noises then said, "Now, we need to go to your place to get your bow. We are going to need to shoot out the lock of the church door. Reckon you can do that?"

I didn't believe my bow was powerful enough for a shot like that, but I grinned, shrugged, and said, "I can't miss!"

We laughed. I fired up the monster and we set off for my house. I glanced at the clock on the dash. It was three a.m. Sun-up in just a few hours.

* * * *

I parked at the end of the drive and sprinted quietly to the front door. I let myself in with my key and crept up the stairs. You can't do that quietly in an old Tudor house, because a Tudor house is a living, breathing—and especially creaking — thing. I spread my legs like a crab and inched up, treading on the outermost part of each step where there was the least movement and made it to the top more or less quietly.

I paused on the landing and listened. I could hear my dad snoring softly, blissfully unaware of the total catastrophe he was going to encounter later that day — his son expelled from school, arrested for grand theft auto, himself in disgrace and his own career threatened by the scandal. I groaned inwardly and crept on, among the house's soft creaks and bumps, to my room. I slipped in and closed the door gently behind me — and stared.

Standing by the window, caught by the last, dim light of the sinking moon, was a six-foot longbow. It was the most beautiful thing I had ever seen, and beside it were three long, sturdy arrows.

I stepped closer and picked it up. It looked like yew, but it was lighter and denser, with a high polish. The handgrip was leather with exquisite runes cut into the hardened skin. As I examined the stave, I saw more runes that seemed to appear and vanish within the wood itself. I strung it and tested the tension. It was immensely powerful, perhaps one hundred pounds draw weight. This was a war bow, more than sufficient to punch out the lock of the church door.

I set it down and picked up the arrows. They were long and firm, also designed for war. They were identical but for their heads. One was an iron bodkin — an armor piercing shaft, designed to punch through armor. The other two were broadheads, but they appeared to be made of gold. I knew exactly what each one was for. I knew then, in my mind, that there would be one more thing for me, and it was there, lying on the bed — a Viking broadsword, identical to the one Dicky had lent me. Hard and bright as diamonds in a wooden scabbard bound in leather. Again, the scabbard and the blade were engraved with runes. Mentally, I thanked Gorm for bringing me the tools I would need to protect Ciara, but even as I did so, I was aware, even as he had told me, that these gifts had not come from Gorm himself, that he was merely the messenger.

I slung them over my shoulder and slipped down the stairs as quietly as I could. I stepped out into the darkest hour and closed the door. The moon was an inch over the horizon, whispering frosted light onto the ancient hills. A cold breeze had risen, and the first chill of coming winter was in the air. I shivered, gripped my bow and my sword and loped along the driveway to the waiting car.

I climbed in and slammed the door behind me. It was warm and muffled inside. I showed Sebastian what I had found. He examined them then shook his head and laughed. "This is a nerd's wet dream, and you're not even a geek."

I laughed, too. "Sheldon Cooper, eat your heart out."

The huge, supercharged V6 roared into life, and we took off toward Little Sodbury. At that time of the morning, the roads were deserted, and I drove with a reckless abandon that, instead of terrifying Sebastian as it did me, seemed to amuse him. Within twelve minutes, we were rumbling back into the town. I pulled up by the commons opposite the church and out of sight then killed the engine. We sat for a couple of minutes, staring across the dark square, with the dull amber lights of the street lamps making the shadows seem deeper and the dead, sleepless eyes of the houses blacker. I heard Sebastian mutter, "Death walks here tonight..." and I knew he was right.

I turned to him. "We'll go to the churchyard gate. You go ahead and hide behind the tombstone closest to the church door. I'll take out the lock and charge the church. Once I'm inside and I engage them, you come in behind. You snatch Ciara and her dad and get out and to the Jag. I'll fight a rearguard, fall back to the car then we go."

He nodded. "That's the plan. Let's do it."

We sprinted across the square and ducked in through the churchyard gate. While I strung the bow, Sebastian threaded his way at a half-run through the graveyard and finally crouched behind a huge stone, maybe fifteen or twenty feet from the church door. When I saw him duck, I nocked the iron bodkin, drew the massive bow, saw the iron keyhole in my mind's eye, knew I would pierce it with the barb and loosed.

Chapter Thirteen

There was a whisper in the night, then a dull metallic thud and a soft creak. I slung the bow over my shoulder and sprinted up the path. As I arrived, I jumped and kicked the door with all my might. I jarred my leg, staggered and fell sprawling. I made the door swing a full two inches. As I hopped around holding my leg and cussing under my breath, Sebastian came running up to me. He ignored me and gently pushed the door a couple of feet farther. He slipped in through the gap and I hobbled after him.

It was real dark inside and silent as a grave. I touched Sebastian's arm and whispered to him to get behind the nearest pew. Then I inched down the aisle toward the altar. Nothing happened until I was halfway along. There was an almighty crash and the door smashed closed. Then all hell broke loose, literally — and I do mean, literally.

Above the altar, a swirling spiral of red and orange flames spinning counterclockwise at a dizzying speed disgorged what I could only describe as a giant lizard man with black and green scaly skin and phosphorescent yellow eyes, wielding a huge trident spear. He was riding a lizard-panther the size of a minibus that sprang at me with its vast maw open and fire spurting from where its eyes should have been. The roar was horrific. I screamed and knew in my bones that it was all over. I was dead.

But I wasn't. Somehow my muscles moved on their own. I was possessed. Somehow my sword was in my hands and I smashed it into the panther's face. It reared, snarling, and the trident came at me from nowhere. I hammered it to one side and slashed at the panther's belly. I know I hurt it because its scream rattled the rafters and it took off up to the ceiling, leaving behind it a trail of sulfur. Flames licked at the ancient beams then it was nose-diving at me and the lizard-man was leaning to his side, holding the trident as a lance. There was a scream like a squadron of F-16s and the air caught fire. My sword seemed to move of its own volition. I batted the lance to one side, spun on my heel, brought the blade smashing down, two-handed, and split the demon lizard-panther right down the middle. I clove it in twain and rendered it asunder. No mistake.

There was a horrific explosion. The screaming and thrashing was unbearable and I collapsed into the fetal position, covering my head with my arms. The ground shook and there was a blast of burning air and a stench of sulfur—then silence. I poked my head out of my arms and looked up. I think I said, "Oh, shit!"

There was no trace of the lizard-panther, but his rider was standing over me. He must have been fifteen-feet-tall if he was an inch. He appeared like he'd been drawn by one of the Marvel team while they were tripping on mescaline. Two massive goat's horns had sprouted from his head and curled all the way down to the backs of his knees. He had a washboard abdomen and muscles no organic being ought to have and in places they ought never be. He had smoke coiling out of his nostrils and in his hand, instead of the trident, he now held a massive hammer.

His roar shook the foundations of the church but his hammer blow shook the foundations of the earth. Something made me roll, and the hit missed me by an inch. If he'd hit me, I would have been atomized. I ran, jumped, ducked and rolled again, and with every move I made, a massive hammer strike fell where I had been half a second before. This was not sword fighting. I could not keep it up indefinitely and I could not get close enough to him to finish it. I was on the defensive and sooner, rather than later, he was going to get me.

I suddenly knew what I had to do. I sprinted to put some

distance between us then I stopped and turned, facing him. I braced myself and waited for the attack. He snarled, bellowed and swung at me back-handed. I parried with my sword in the last second. The force lifted me and threw me twenty feet. I landed with a crash and slid another fifteen feet, spinning on the stone floor as I went. Finally, I hit the wall and stopped. I was winded and gasping, and my chest felt like it was going to rip in half. The great demon was standing, bellowing a huge laugh that threatened to bring down the roof. I had no time to watch or feel sorry for myself. Every micro-second counted. I dropped my sword and pulled the bow from my back. In another second, I had one of the gold-tipped arrows and I had nocked it and pulled. He froze, staring with wild eyes. He moved too late. I had loosed. There was a whisper in the air and the arrow met its mark in the dead center of his heart.

The explosion was a white, nuclear blast, and the scream that went with it was harrowing. It was the despair of a demon cast back into the black void of Hell. It passed, and next I was lying on my back, trembling. There was an eerie, unearthly glow in the air. I turned and saw Sebastian still crouching behind the pew. He appeared ashen. I heard his voice like it was coming from a million miles away. "That's what you call a *leprechaun*?"

I struggled to my feet. "Whatever they are, there is another one. Wait—"

Far at the other end of the church, beyond the altar, a door banged open with a reverberating echo and two men burst through. They seemed to be miles away, striding toward me. The nearest was lean, dressed in black, with a cloak hanging from his shoulders. He had an authoritative, almost aristocratic, bearing. The man behind him was big, muscular. He gave the impression of a bear, with a huge fur cloak and a great battle-ax over his shoulder. Dicky had arrived with the other shape-shifting leprechaun.

I staggered to my feet and held my sword in both hands. I knew exactly what I had to do. I fixed Dicky with my eyes and clamped my mind on him vise-like. I saw him break his stride and falter. His right hand went to his head. I hit him like a sledge hammer, plunging in and bellowing into his mind, "*What do you want? Tell me! What do you want?*" Then I visualized my mind was a vacuum, sucking everything from inside him. I felt my stomach clench and my mouth open, and I roared like a demented ogre as I dragged his thoughts from his head.

He stopped, bent almost double, both hands to his temples. His eyes were clenched shut as he screamed, "*Nooooo!*"

I let go and, before he could recover, I charged him. I pelted six strides, then I leaped as he staggered back and I smashed into his chest with both feet. He went flying and crashed into the hairy hulk behind him. They both sprawled on the floor. Before they had time to think, my blade was flashing left and right. They cowered under their raised weapons, half-sitting, struggling to get to their feet. I bombarded them with blows, and all the while, I fastened my mind on Dicky, sucking on his thoughts, blitzing his brain with mine. I am pretty sure he had never experienced an assault like it in his life.

I had no idea what Sebastian was doing. I blocked him firmly from my thoughts so that there was no chance of Dicky's realizing what the real attack was and that I was just a diversion. And Sebastian was as good as his word because he skidded as he reached the chancel and ducked to his left in front of the altar, heading for the door through which Dicky and the hulk had appeared. He had no choice but to do that, because it was the only way down to the crypt. But it was a shame because just for that moment I saw him, and just for a fraction of a second, I faltered. That was all Dicky needed.

He'd caught it. In a flash, he rolled, spun and kicked my legs from under me. I smashed onto my back and the wind was knocked from my lungs. My chest went into spasm, and as hard as I gasped, I couldn't get any air into my lungs. He sprang to his feet and raised the sword in both hands, its tip pointing straight down at my heart, and he plunged.

My hand moved of its own volition. My blade flashed, and as I rasped for air, I deflected his blow and it hit the granite floor in a shower of sparks. I staggered to my feet, screeching for air. Six blows rained on me from his blade and I parried them all while clawing at my throat. Then I saw it. My heart leaped with terror and I screamed, "*Noooo!*"

Sebastian was hurtling like a quarterback on speed toward the door of the crypt. He was reaching for the handle, but just inches behind him was the hairy hulk. I sprang forward toward them, but Dicky kicked me in the shins and I sprawled on my face. As I slid forward, I saw the big hulk grab Sebastian by the back of his neck and yank hard. Sebastian was lifted off his feet and flew backward toward the chancel. He hit the stone floor on his back, bounced and somersaulted like a rag doll and flopped face down on the floor. He lay motionless. I felt sick.

The great brute raised his hammer over his head. I sprang to my feet with a yelp, sideswiped Dicky with my sword and leaped. I brought my blade up as his hammer was crashing down. The blow jarred me to the bone, but if Sebastian wasn't already dead, it saved his life. I cut savagely down and gashed the hulk's leg. He staggered back. I spun and raised my sword over my head without thinking. It stopped Dicky's blade splitting my skull. His midriff was wide open so I kicked him hard in the belly, and as he went down, I kicked him again, twice. When he rolled and scrambled to his feet, I turned and hammered at the hulk with six lightning-fast blows of my sword. He fell and that gave me three seconds. I turned and probed Sebastian's mind with mine. He was sick and numb, but he was alive. I blasted him with the command, "*Crawl to the door to the crypt! I will cover you!*"

And they were on me with a hail of blows. My sword moved at warp speed. Wherever the stabs or slashes came from, my sword was there — deflecting, parrying, blocking. I made no effort to strike back. That would waste energy.

All I wanted was to cover Sebastian as he crawled, inch by agonizing inch, to the door through which Dicky had arrived. And while I defended myself, I probed Dicky's mind again—attacking, sucking at his thoughts, draining him of his concentration. My mind locked on his skull, hammering and grinding its way in. He was staring and the sweat was running down his brow. I inched back two steps, feeling for Sebastian with my heel. He had moved.

Then I heard the creak of the door. Dicky heard it, too, and his eyes widened in a glare. He knew, suddenly, that he had been tricked. He roared like a lion and redoubled his attack. But he knew, as I did, that I was invincible, as was he, and as long as I was just defending myself, there was nothing he could do. Meanwhile, behind me, Sebastian was dragging himself to his feet, leaning on the door jamb. Now, I needed to turn the tables. Now, I needed to go on the offensive.

I launched a savage, unstoppable attack on the hulk, forcing Dicky to come to his defense. I nicked his cheek, slashed his leg and cut his arm, my blade moving faster than the eye could see. He reeled and backed away as Dicky fought desperately to deflect my blows. Then I turned on him and lunged with my blade at his face, and simultaneously, with my mind, I seized his brain and rammed a nuclear bomb into his imagination. It exploded in an insane, white flash. He screamed and stepped back, gripping his head with his hands. I turned. Sebastian was down the first three steps. The door stood open. I stepped in. The last thing I saw before I slammed it was Dicky's raging face, and in that moment, for a fraction of a second, I read something in his eyes. I turned the key and we were in absolute darkness.

I could hear Sebastian's ragged breathing a couple of feet from me. I said, "You okay?"

His voice came back, trembling but reassuring. "Don't be ridiculous."

I felt in my pocket and pulled out my cell. I switched on

the flashlight app and saw his face shying away from the glare. We inched our way down the steps. After a minute of slow progress, we came to the bottom. There was a kind of small lobby with a door on the right and a door on the left. I was wondering why the hulk hadn't just ripped the door off its hinges and followed us down, but he hadn't, and that was enough for me. I stood a moment and calculated where the window was that I had peered through. I crossed to the door on the right, pushed it open and saw the most horrific sight I have ever seen in my life.

Ciara was sitting on a sofa, trembling and sobbing. Michael Fionn was sitting next to her with his arm around her. His face was drawn and gray. They both looked up as we pushed in. Then we all stared at the padre, lying on the floor, staring sightlessly at the ceiling with a dagger stuck in his heart.

Ciara turned back to me. She was shaking her head and tears were streaming down her cheeks. She said, "He tried to protect us."

Her dad scowled at me. "I suppose you've come to finish the job."

Ciara grabbed his arm in her hands. "No, Dad. This is Jake. I told you about him. He's come to rescue us."

I heard Sebastian's wry, exhausted voice over my shoulder. "And I'm Sebastian, also here to rescue you."

Fionn said, "And how the bloody hell do you plan to do that?"

Sebastian placed a hand on my shoulder and leaned heavily on me. "Yes, Jake, mannerless and ungrateful as the bugger is, I have to concur. How the bloody hell do we plan to do that? There is one way out of here and that is blocked by a hairy Viking and an immoderate twat."

Fionn scowled some more and said, "I'll not let you put my girl at risk."

Ciara said, "Oh, for God's sake, Daddy!"

And Sebastian said, "You might make it through, Jake, but the rest of us don't stand a chance. We'll be slaughtered in seconds."

I spoke quietly. "If you'll all please just shut the fuck up, I'll tell you how."

Chapter Fourteen

"There is a secret exit through the crypt—a priest hole or something, from the Reformation. But we have to be quick. They might know I know by now."

Michael Fionn examined me suspiciously. "How do you know that?"

I glanced at Sebastian. He just barely perceptibly shook his head. Ciara was watching me curiously.

I said, "It's hard to explain, but I managed to get a look at some old documents."

Sebastian said, "Lay on, McDuff... Let's get out of here. I, for one, have had enough."

We stepped out of the small room and into the makeshift lobby, and there we took the other door that had been on our left and was now on our right. It was a huge, ancient oak thing shaped in a Norman arch. There was an old iron key in it. I turned and pulled. The wood had swollen and warped, but after a few shoves, it grated open.

It was pitch black in the crypt. I fished out my cell. The battery was at half. The flashlight app really chewed up the charge, but we had to use it. The shadows seemed to spring back into the corners. It was a kind of a honeycomb of Norman arches under a vaulted ceiling. It appeared like sandstone but it was hard to tell. I played the light around and the darkness seemed to scurry away here as it closed in there. There was a soft echo of scratching feet.

I whispered, "Come on," and Sebastian closed the door behind us.

Fionn, voice harsh in the blackness, asked, "Well, where is this famous tunnel, then?"

I said, "I'm not sure... Somewhere down there."

I pointed with the beam of the flashlight and he said, "That's just brilliant."

We shuffled, picking our way through the impenetrable gloom, huddled in the small pool of light cast by my phone. The ancient arches and columns seemed to lean in and scowl at us as we passed.

Fionn rasped, "I hate rats! Where in God's name are you leading us?"

I didn't bother answering. I was concentrating too hard on trying to see what was ahead while trying to fix on what I had snatched from Dicky when he'd realized he'd been foiled — when he'd realized we were going down into the crypt. He had not looked triumphant, as he should have if he'd had us trapped down here. He seemed enraged — even fearful. And in that unguarded moment, I had read his mind. There was a tunnel, it was here and I had snatched a picture from his thoughts. It was a picture of us, going through a concealed door.

The far wall rose before us. I played the beam over it. There was no door, but there wouldn't be, not a visible one. *What had he seen? Where, exactly, had he seen us?*

"Well?" It was Fionn.

I heard Ciara sigh. "Dad, please."

"I don't want to be trapped and die down here at the hands of this incompetent whelp!"

"Dad!"

"Don't feckin' 'Dad' me! I'll have the police on this lot of —"

Sebastian's cool voice cut right across him like a frozen razor. "Shut up, Mr. Fionn. If you don't, I promise you that if Jake doesn't cut your throat, I will. Do we understand each other? Shut up and do as you're told."

I thought I heard Ciara snigger, but aside from that, there was only silence, and in that silence, I saw it. I stepped over to the wall, ran my hand over a few of the massive sandstone bricks, found the one and pushed. There was a loud rumbling of stone and a six-foot section of the wall rolled back.

If the crypt was pitch-black, this was whatever comes next on the scale of darkness. I shone the light in and saw it was a narrow tunnel, just wide enough for one person, with steps cut out of the living limestone. I turned and shone the light at them. Ciara and Sebastian screwed up their eyes and Fionn covered his with his hand.

I said, "Okay, we're going down. Follow me, slowly and carefully."

The walls and the steps were damp and slippery, and the tunnel curved slightly to the right so that progress was tedious. A few feet ahead of us was perpetually in the dark. It was hard to keep track of time. But after a while, the steps became steeper and the tunnel straightened so that I could see maybe fifteen or twenty feet ahead. Now it was becoming a perilous slope, and we had to hold on to the walls to avoid slipping and falling.

Then the walls fell away.

We were in a vast cavern. It was impossible to see what lay on either side of us or ahead. I heard Fionn exclaim behind me, "Sweet mother of God! Jesus, Mary and sweet Joanna! Where in God's name—?"

I interrupted him and said, "Be quiet!"

"Don't feckin' tell me to be—"

"Shut *up!*" It was Ciara.

In the silence that followed her voice, you could just make out the sigh, lap and whisper of water.

I said, "We're at an underground river."

"And now what?" It was Fionn again.

I said, "Sit down. The steps are slimy and there's nothing to hold on to. We'll go down on our butts."

I was shining the light into the void, trying to make out shapes, trying to see where the water was. Behind me, I could hear Fionn still expostulating, but I was trying to ignore him. That was a mistake. I should have been paying closer attention, but I wasn't.

Somewhere in my peripheral hearing he was saying, "I will *not* sit on wet stone! You must be out of your tiny minds!"

I guess he'd had enough of being bossed, scared and humiliated, and now he was going to take charge and be in control again. Whatever the reason, he did something real stupid. Suddenly, too late, I was paying attention.

He was saying, "Get out of my way. Let me through. Come on, Ciara. I'll get us out of this hellhole."

I was turning, shouting, "*No!*"

In the beam of my flashlight, I saw Ciara snatching her hand from his grasp. Fionn stepped forward. He nudged me. I felt my balance going and crouched to drop my center of gravity and grip the step. I saw his foot slip and the look of terror on his face as he flailed his arms. I reached and grabbed for his jacket, but it was too late. He was falling. He took three tottering steps past me, slipped and fell screaming into the blackness. Over his scream I heard Ciara's, "Daddyyyy!"

It echoed around the dark emptiness of the cavern and my heart broke at the grief I heard in her voice. There was a loud splash and my heart leaped with hope. I scrambled down the steps, shining the light desperately ahead of me. Then I saw it, the smooth oily swirling of reflected light, and in the midst of it, a black, bobbing head. I turned and rammed the phone into Ciara's hand. "Shine it for me!" And I jumped, not knowing what was beneath me.

As it turned out, I landed about twelve steps below on a small, pebbly beach. I could feel the water lapping at my feet, and in the light that Ciara was shining on the river, I could see Fionn spluttering about ten feet out. I put down my sword and bow then dived in. The water was freezing and deep, but the current wasn't too strong. I surfaced just next to him.

He was half-screaming, half-gasping and kept repeating, "I can't swim! I can't swim!"

As he bobbed and spluttered, I eased behind him and

grabbed him under his shoulders. Then I leaned away with him lying helpless with his back on my chest. I gripped him hard so he wouldn't move and started to maneuver toward the shore, swimming against the current. After a few moments, my feet found the bottom, but it was slippery rock and I couldn't get any purchase. Fionn was beginning to panic and struggle, grunting and thrashing. I wanted to call to Sebastian to come and help me, but Fionn was kicking so much that every time I opened my mouth, it flooded with water and I began to choke. My head went under. I kicked, but I couldn't keep my footing and Fionn's wild jerking was pushing me deeper. Through the water, I could hear muffled shouting. My lungs were screaming and the cold was making my chest go into spasm. I should have let him go and saved myself, but he was Ciara's father, and I'd rather drown than cause her pain.

In a last, desperate attempt, I squeezed my arms in a massive bear hug. Panic gave me a strength I didn't know I had, and I crushed all the air out of his lungs. He went limp and I surfaced, gasping and shouting for air. On the shore, I saw Sebastian reaching out for me, gripping on to Ciara, who was shining my cell-phone flashlight at us. I kicked my feet until I was close enough for him to grab Fionn, and as they dragged him off me, I pulled myself out onto the sodden gravel and collapsed, panting and gasping.

I vomited water a couple of times then pushed myself up onto my knees, locating my bow and sword. Sebastian was slapping Fionn's face, perhaps a little more forcefully than was necessary, and as Fionn groaned and came to, Ciara crouched down next to me.

"Are you okay?"

I nodded. My teeth were chattering. "The water's freezing, but I'll be all right."

She touched my face and the sun came out over a meadow where bluebirds were singing over tulips. She said, "Thank you."

I smiled as manfully as I could and said, "Hey, the bill's in the post," but I winked to show I didn't mean it.

She laughed then went serious. "Whatever it is, Jake, I'll pay it gladly. You're amazing."

Fortunately, it was too dark for her to see the look of absolute idiocy on my face in that moment. And exactly then the flashlight on my cell began to fade. She glanced down at it and said, "It's the battery. It's dying."

I said, "Have you got your cell?"

She shook her head. "Mine and my dad's are upstairs. They were taken from us, obviously."

"Sebastian, have you got your cell?"

He turned to face me. Behind him, Michael Fionn had his knees drawn up and had buried his face in his hands. Sebastian said, "Yes, but there's no signal down here."

"Have you got a flashlight app?"

"No."

"Shit!" I stood and took the phone from Ciara. By its fading light, I could see that to my right, upstream, where Fionn had fallen in, there was a sharp bend and the roof of the cavern sloped toward the ground. To the left, downstream, the cavern roof rose out of sight and the river broadened. On our bank, the pebble beach also broadened and, just on the edge of visibility, I could make out a dark bulk. I pointed. "This leads somewhere. We go this way. We'll use the phone till the battery dies then we'll use your cell, Sebastian. Just use a screen that gives off a pale light. It'll have to do."

He nodded. "Google."

I smiled. "Yeah, Google. Now stay close, everyone — Indian file and hold on to each other."

The light on my cell lasted maybe twenty seconds then died. The blackness was absolute. I heard Sebastian's steady voice behind me saying, "Okay, stay calm, chaps..." and seconds later, a faint light filtered out from the white Google page on the screen of his cell.

It is incredible how, in a matter of a few seconds, your reality can change. One moment, big problems were how I might bring shame and humiliation to my dad, maybe ruin his career, how I might get kicked out of school or arrested for stealing a car and the next, the most important thing in my life was a tiny cell phone. Our whole existence – literally, our whole survival – hinged on this tiny thing I would otherwise take for granted and how much charge it had in the battery. Sebastian handed it to Fionn, who held it like it was the most precious thing he had ever held in his life. He passed it to Ciara, who took it in both hands and handed it to me.

It barely illuminated two feet in front of us. But by its dim light, we shuffled step by careful step forward, toward that indistinct bulk I had seen earlier.

The beach had been narrowing for a while, to the point where I could feel the cavern wall on my left brushing my shoulder and the water of the slow-moving river lapping and squelching under my feet on my right. I was beginning to worry, because I knew that if there was a way out, it had to be along here, downstream. However, it looked like we were running out of dry land, and with it, places to walk. But at the same time, I was certain that if we could press on a bit longer, we had to come to something. Whatever that dark bulk had been that I had seen with my cell just before it had died was our way out. I knew it. Everything depended on our being able to press on.

The ground under my feet began to change from loose, crunching pebbles to bigger, rounder rocks. And the bigger, rounder rocks were also more uneven and more slippery. In the slight glow from Sebastian's phone, each step became slower and more difficult. And that was when, with Ciara hanging on to my shirt behind me, my foot slipped, I over-balanced and crashed down on the rocks. I was rolling, slipping, and I knew I was going to fall into the river. Instinctively I scrabbled with my fingers at the slimy stones, and in doing so, let go of the phone. I didn't fall into the river, but as I caught myself, I heard a quiet plop – and the light went out.

It was pitch-black and deathly silent. After a second, I heard Cara's voice, frightened and uncertain. "Jake?"

I said, "I'm okay. Is everybody there? Everybody okay?"

There was a small chorus of reply in which I counted Sebastian, Michael Fionn and Ciara. I said, "I am going to feel my way to my feet again. Sebastian, have you got Michael?"

"Yes."

"Michael, have you got Ciara?"

"Yes, yes I have."

"Okay, Ciara, you are really close to me. I am going to stand then I want you to reach forward until you can touch me. Okay?"

"Okay."

Until I experienced absolute blackness in a place that was threatening and hostile and totally unfamiliar, it was impossible to have an idea what that would feel like. And 'feel' was the key word. Because there was no sight at all and my hearing was totally deceptive and misleading, all I had was the sense of touch. I groped carefully to my left until I felt the cavern wall, then I felt my way up the wall until I was standing. Then I said, "Ciara?"

"Yes."

She sounded real close and I put out my left hand, back toward where I had heard her. I said, "Reach out toward me and keep talking."

"I'm here. I'm trying to find you. I can't feel you…"

I took a small step toward her, groping in the dark, but I couldn't find her, either. "You're real close, Ciara. I can hear you are real close. Keep feeling. Inch toward my voice, keep your arm outstretched and sweep slowly. That's what I'm doing. We have to find each other that way."

While I was saying that, she was talking, too. "I'm reaching for you, but I can't—"

Somehow, our hands had missed, and suddenly, our bodies were touching. I could feel her breath on my face, and her lips right next to mine. We froze, but we didn't move away. And there, in the absolute darkness, we caressed each other's faces, first with our hands then, impossibly gentle, with our lips. Then we came together, locked in a sublime, eternal kiss. I have no idea how long we stayed that way and I didn't care, because for me it lasted—and would last—forever.

Eventually we became aware of voices, Sebastian's and Fionn's, asking, "What's happened? Have you found him?"

Ciara said, with a huge smile in her voice, "Yes, I found him," and I turned and began to feel my way again, with the hugest, most idiotic grin on my face that anyone, anywhere, could ever have.

We carried on for another five minutes or so, which in absolute blackness feels like an eternity, then the rocks gave way again to pebbles, and the beach expanded into a broad, flat area. The sound of the water changed, too, and became faster and louder, with more echo, as though the cavern had opened out. We moved along a little quicker, with more confidence, and something inside told me this was the place—the place where I had seen the dark shape.

And that was when I smashed my shin, slipped, fell sprawling and cracked my head. When I had finished swearing and was struggling to get back to my feet, I heard Ciara calling out to me, "Jake? Jake? Are you okay? Where are you?"

And over her, Fionn was saying, "What now? What the feck is happening now?"

And Sebastian, "Jake? Jake? Ciara, what's happened?"

And I froze in a crumpled heap. "Be quiet, all of you!"

"What?"

I began to laugh, groping around me, feeling the damp, worn wood. "I've fallen into a boat!" I shouted. "I'm touching timber. I'm in a rowboat!"

Chapter Fifteen

The others managed to grope their way to the boat and Sebastian and I pushed it out into the current. Then we scrambled aboard—which isn't easy in absolute blackness— amid scratches and bruises and much swearing. We couldn't see a damned thing, but there were oars in the boat, and instead of using them to move us along—the current was taking us at a nice, languid pace—we used them to keep us from hitting the cavern walls. And we bumped along like this, drifting, with no sense of what direction we were moving in or the passage of time. Ten minutes might have passed or it might have been half an hour or an hour. The fact is, when you can see nothing, it becomes almost impossible to gauge time. But eventually Ciara said what we had all probably been thinking, without daring to say it.

"The darkness is lessening. It isn't so...black."

I nodded, which was stupid because nobody could see me. "I think you're right."

We carried on like that for another good few minutes, each of us straining our eyes to try to pierce the gloom, bobbing to the gentle lapping of the stream with no real sense of movement or direction. Then I saw it, like a ghost through the grainy, dark air. It was mere feet away.

I said, "I can see bricks. The wall. It's red brick. It isn't stone."

And Ciara was talking at the same time, saying, "Yes! You're right. We're in a tunnel. It's not a cave anymore."

Then there was light, filtering in from somewhere, dim and gray and dull. But it was light. And while Michael Fionn was thanking the good Lord and all the saints, I noticed up ahead, a small jetty, also made of brick, and beyond it some stone steps leading up through an arch. I pointed. "There! There! Row, row, row!"

And Sebastian and I began to haul on the oars, nosing the little boat toward the mooring. When we'd secured it and climbed out, I slung my sword and my bow over my shoulder. Fionn was babbling like he had verbal diarrhea, thanking us and preparing to say his and Cara's goodbyes. I wasn't really listening. I was thinking about how there was still one gold-tipped arrow left. I looked at Ciara. She was watching me. I said, "We're not there yet."

She nodded. "I know…"

I led the way up the stairs.

It was a narrow tunnel again, just wide enough for one person. The stairs were steep, made of limestone and worn down in the middle, as if they'd had centuries of use. We climbed in single file for maybe ten minutes, and finally up ahead, I saw the dim glow of filtered light. Another minute brought us to the head of the stairs. We were in a circular room with a dirt floor. It seemed to be some kind of a tower, with a high, domed ceiling supported by stone arches. The door was also arched, though this arch seemed more Tudor than Norman. It was made of heavy wood that might have been oak, but it was cracked and uncared for and the light of early dawn was filtering through it. There was a large iron key in the lock, and I thought at the time that this was strange. I took hold of the key, turned and pushed then stepped through into the light.

Only it wasn't light. It was still night. We were in what appeared to be the ruins of an old abbey. The walls were broken and crumbling. There was no roof, and above us there was a clear, translucent sky with a full silver moon, gently raining light over rolling hills and hedgerows. I could hear an owl calling from somewhere across the dark fields, and there was the rich smell of honeysuckle and nocturnal roses on the air.

I noticed Ciara standing next to me. She gently slipped

her arm through mine. Her father appeared by her side, mumbling. I glanced down at him and his eyes were drooping. He seemed half asleep. And just past him, I saw Sebastian. He didn't seem much better. He was yawning hugely and struggling to keep his eyes open. He put an arm around Fionn and said, "Come on. Let's find somewhere to sit down, old chap."

Ciara pointed ahead of us and said, "Look. We can sit by that fire and keep warm for the night."

Am I dreaming? But I knew I wasn't, even though time seemed to have gone backward. In a dream you can see and you can hear, but you can't feel. And I could feel everything perfectly.

I turned toward where she was pointing, and I saw that there was a ring of stones, maybe four feet across, and in the center, there was a fire burning, trailing a few sparks into the night air. I hadn't seen it before, but that didn't strike me as strange, given everything else.

We walked over to it and sat. Sebastian and Fionn lay down, curled up and were instantly in a deep asleep. I listened to the crackle of the flames consuming the wood for a while and enjoyed their warmth on my skin. I turned to Ciara. She was very close, watching me intently, and her eyes were alive with reflected flames.

"I know about the debate, Jake."

I laughed, and there was a strange echo among the walls of the ancient abbey. "I don't stand a chance. They'll expel me, I'm sure. It will be hard on my dad, but I had to do what I did. I couldn't let them take you."

She smiled. The warm glow of the fire bathed her skin, and I had the strange feeling that the warmth was coming out from her, from her heart. She said, "There are things you still don't understand. I didn't understand myself until tonight. I want you to promise me something. Will you do something for me?"

I smiled. "What do you think?"

She took my hand in both of hers. "I want you to promise

me that you will do the debate. I know you've prepared nothing, and that's good, because I want you to speak from the heart. More than that, Jake, I want you to allow your heart to speak. Will you do that for me?"

"I would do anything for you, Ciara."

She gave a small laugh, which I am not going to describe because I'd have to say things like the tinkling of silver bells, and I refuse to do that. But I will say it was a laugh that would make a skylark go weak at the knees — if skylarks have knees, that is.

Then she said, "Thank you, my Lord, and I will make my father come and listen to you, because he needs to hear what your heart has to say. Now" — I was about to speak, but she placed a finger on my lips and said — "I must sleep a while, and you must stay awake and alert. The biggest battle is yet to come."

She closed her eyes, her head dropped forward and, in an instant, she was deeply asleep and I was alone.

It was a strange feeling, and that was what it was — a feeling. As I searched about me, I noticed that all the colors were more intense than I had ever seen them before. The orange and yellow of the fire were luminous. The black, charred logs from which the flames licked and reached up into the air were of a blackness I had never seen. The grass where I was sitting from which the crumbling walls of the abbey rose, was almost electric, shimmering, and the amber yellow of the sandstone walls seemed to glow with an inner light. I looked up and the depth of the blue of the night sky was like polished glass. The stars were tiny shards of ice, and against that backdrop, the moon seemed to be a living thing, with a radiance more intense than the sun. Yet it was dark, and the intensity of these colors radiated from that darkness so strongly that it was more than color. It was feeling. That is the only way I could explain it. Every color and every shape was a feeling. The sky and the stars were icy cold, the abbey walls were ancient and tired, the green of the grass was young and wild and mischievous and the silver light of the moon was secret and timeless – and maybe even amused.

I knew that there were questions I ought to be asking – like how the hell we had walked into an abbey at midnight when it was dawn as I was opening the door – but the strangest feeling of all was the one that said that those questions did not matter. Who questions what they do in a dream? Well, this was like being awake in a dream that was more real than reality.

I'm not sure when I first saw it... One minute it was not there, then it was. But it was there as though it had always been there. It's really hard to explain. It was sitting across the fire from me, with the light from the flames reflecting in orange and green and purple off its scales and dancing in its huge eyes. It was human-shaped, more or less, sitting in a half-lotus position. Its face was long, with a pointed snout, like a goat with no ears, and though the face and body appeared quite masculine, it had two very feminine breasts. I must have seemed surprised, because it said, in a deep, masculine voice, "Did you think you were alone, Jay En?"

I looked around at Ciara, Michael Fionn and Sebastian, all sleeping. And it said, "They are not here."

I turned back to face it, and it was like I'd held a magnifying glass over its eyes. They were vast and right there in front of me, two giant goat's eyes staring right down deep inside me. I pushed the image back with my mind and said, "Who are you?"

It was reptilian. It had no face muscles, so it couldn't smile, but there was real humor in its eyes. "I am Naga."

I had a million questions I wanted to ask, but I couldn't find words for any of them. I said, "Why are you here, Naga?"

It opened its mouth, like a Komodo Dragon, threw back its head and brayed loudly, like an ass. A huge, multicolored crest of spines and scales spread out from behind its neck, and its skin seemed to ripple with colors. It stopped, the crest sank back and it gazed at me, while its forked tongue licked the air.

"Why? An impossible question to answer, Jay En. The only answer to 'why' is 'because'. How do I come to be here? This is my home, as it is yours. What is my purpose? To speak to you. Learn, young being, to ask *good* questions."

"Why do you want to –?"

"Again?"

I stopped and drew breath. "What is it that you want to talk to me about?"

"You must speak about Earth, about our world."

"I must?"

He watched me, like he was waiting for me to realize how stupid I was. Then the penny dropped. "Oh, you're talking about the debate!"

"You must speak about Earth, about the world we share."

The silence was suddenly intense. It was as though there was a furious noise just outside my range of hearing. Naga's eyes became huge again.

I heard myself repeating in a monotone, "The world we share."

"Did you think you were alone?"

I frowned, straining. Something was knocking at the door of my memory. I said, "*Naga*... Hindu mythology..."

Again, he asked, "Did you think you were alone? There are many rooms in the mansion of the world. If you stepped into the sky, Jay En, and surveyed the world with my eyes, you would see the many rivers and streams, and oceans of the mind, flowing from flower to butterfly, to lark to goat, to man, to elf to naga."

And as he spoke, I realized that I was in space, looking down on our planet, but as I had never seen it in any photograph from NASA. It was a luminous ball, shrouded in the most fantastical mist of billions upon billions of colors. And each color was a stream or a river or a lake or an ocean, and they were all moving, entwining. And Naga was saying, "Each stream, Jay En, is a stream of conscious thought. Some are feeble and slow and sluggish, and they you see as gray or brown. Others are wild and furious, full of hunger and rage, and those you see in red or purple. Others are full of love and fertility, and those you see in pink and violet and green. Some, Jay En, are just feeling, like the yellows and greens of flowers, whose consciousness is simple, yet rich in feeling. Others crawl in the dark, like cockroaches seeking food, and these are also simple, blacks and grays and browns and shadow colors. Humans you will see in the whole, fantastic spectrum from black, murderous hatred to glorious, shining love and compassion but almost always tinged with the darkness of ignorance, believing themselves still to be masters — at best, caretakers — of this world.

"But open your eyes and see clearly, Jay En, and you will see more subtle streams of colors, and these are the thousands of lives that are not human but whose consciousness reaches far beyond human dreams. We share this world, Jay En, and we love it as humans do not yet know how to. We do not kill, torture and punish. We wait, and we try to teach. Sometimes we send a great teacher among the humans, to guide their steps, and sometimes we send a small teacher. Each teacher, great and small, has an equally important part to play.

"And so, Jay En, you must talk about Earth."

We were sitting around the fire again. I could feel the warmth of the flames on my skin, and I could see the orange and yellow dancing on Naga's scaly skin. There was a smile in its eyes.

I said, "What about Ar En?"

"One day, you will learn to ask questions that find answers. Ar En is your brother. He is your mirror. There are many forms of intelligent life in the world, young being. Some are motivated by love, like us. Others are motivated by confusion, like the humans. Yet others are motivated by anger and lust. You must be careful of them. But all are your brothers and sisters, and all are your mirrors, for they can teach you about yourself when you look into their hearts."

I was beginning to feel a turmoil in my mind. I frowned at him and said, "Who are you?"

And in spite of its rigid, lizard face, it was smiling, and it seemed to be turning to smoke. Its voice came to me through the flames of the fire, which was growing and spreading. It said, "I told you, young being, I am Naga. Did you *really* think you were alone?

Quietly, the fire crackled. A few sparks drifted across the luminous green grass. The broken walls watched me, gently glowing amber in the moonlight. Naga was not there, and I wondered if I had dreamed it. In the stillness, I saw the broken arch of the main entrance to the abbey. A hooded figure in a black shroud stood watching me. By his side was a huge dog, which he held on a short chain.

A voice that I recognized, that I knew well, echoed around the abbey, strong in power and authority. "I have come to ask you a question, Jay."

I got to my feet. My sheathed sword weighed on my back. I held the bow with the one remaining arrow in my left hand. The night air was suddenly cold on my skin and the fire burned low. I spoke, but it was more of a snarl. "Ask…"

"Do you support the dominion of man? Will you, as your father's son, cower at their feet, feed them our blood and hold the torch while they scorch our world and drive us into the shadows? Or will you, as your mother's son, fight them and drive them back into the frozen blackness of the night from which they came? Do you, Jay, my brother, support the dominion of man?"

He pushed back his hood. An icy wind blew and caught his shroud, blowing it like a black cape. He was my brother, my mirror, but as I had not seen him before. He was no high-school boy. He was ancient beyond measure, tall and proud and beautiful in a way that no human could understand. He was the earth, he was the trees and the grass and the rivers, and for a while, I felt the tug of his words. I understood him and felt a fury and a rage against this upstart species that was destroying our world, burning the air with their smog, murdering, raping, enslaving, spreading darkness over our home.

But even as I felt these things, the passion subsided and clarity came to me. I said, "It is not the dominion of man, Ar. It is the dominion of hate, and hate already has dominion over your heart. I do not support the dominion of hate, and so I will not fight them and drive them back into the dark. I will lend them what little light I have, to help them to see the beauty of their home, share it with us and grow from man to humanity. Will you, my brother, help me to bring them light?"

He seemed to freeze, to go rigid, then his whole body appeared to grow. His face blazed with a furious fire. The sky turned black with turbulent clouds. Lightning crackled and a furious wind tore through the abbey, whipping his hair across his face. He opened his mouth and roared, *"Never by Dagda and Lugh! By Odin and Fjörgyn! May Vritra scorch the earth before I will be a friend to Manu!"*

And so saying, he let slip his hound. It sprang from his grasp with burning eyes, baring its massive teeth. And in the same instant, he had a bow in his hand and he had loosed two flaming arrows straight at my heart.

Chapter Sixteen

My sword once again moved of its own volition. I had it suddenly in my right hand and batted away the arrows as though they were nothing more than annoying, sluggish flies. Then I tossed it in the air, and as it spun above me, I nocked my last remaining arrow, pulled and loosed, and the golden-tipped barb struck home into the hound's heart. It exploded in a flash of purple and violet light with a terribly baying howl. I dropped the bow, held out my right hand and my sword dropped into it with a solid thud.

Ar En was in the air, Chinese kung fu warrior style, with his sword over his head. I leaped to meet him, and somehow, we had bridged the hundred yards between us. Our swords crashed in a shower of sparks, and as we landed, he swung at my legs. I jumped over his blade and brought my own crashing down at his skull. He avoided it easily and for the next ten minutes we rained blows on each other like two crazed demons. We defied gravity and all the laws of physics. We sprang to the highest peaks on the wall. We smashed through ancient stone. We did somersaults thirty feet in the air. Our blades moved at the speed of light, but still it was impossible for either of us to land a single blow or draw a single drop of blood.

Then, suddenly, the stupidity of the whole thing struck me and I rammed the blade of my sword into the turf and shouted at him, "Stop!"

He came to rest in front of me with a smile that might have been a sneer. He said, "Do you surrender, Jay?"

I shook my head. "This is absurd. Neither of us can defeat the other. Why this hatred? Why can't we be brothers?"

He raised his sword and leveled the blade at me. "Because you serve the enemy of Mother Earth. Because your blood is tainted with their blood. Because they rape and murder Danu, even as they rape and murder each other, and yet you make them your friends and serve them."

"What are you *talking* about?"

He roared and brought his blade double-handed down toward my head. I blocked him with bare inches to spare. He hammered over and over again, and with each blow, he spat words at me. "They. Must. Be. Banished! They. Must. Be. Cast. Back!"

And as he struck at me, I shouted at him, "Stop! Stop! Back where? I don't know what you're talking about!"

He stopped, but his face was a mask of fury and his eyes were on fire. He raised his sword, pointed it into my face and bellowed, "Death! I am talking about death! The murder of our Mother Earth! The rape and murder of the spirit that gives us life! I am talking about you! You and your betrayal!"

"What betrayal? For crying out loud, talk sense! Who have I betrayed?"

There was silence as he stared at me and slowly his expression changed. "You really don't know, do you? You don't remember anything. You truly are a young being."

Now it was he who stabbed his sword into the turf. He stepped toward me until we were just a couple of feet apart. Then he reached out with his right hand and placed it over my heart.

He said, "You are of the blood of the elven folk who walked this world long before man came with his war machines and his black heart. They have driven us from our woodlands and our mountain homes. They have driven us from the rivers and the glens, until the whole world is full of their smoke and the ugly banging of their iron machines. And some of us, Jay, believe it is time to take our home back and return these mad creatures into the blackness from which they came." He was silent a moment, staring deep into my eyes. "But, you," he said at last, "you count them as our friends. You take it as our destiny to walk with them and hold them close to your heart, as others have done before you. You do not remember, but you will."

And with that, he twisted his hand and pulled, smiled and held before me the medallion that I had worn around my neck since that first day when I'd seen Gorm—the amulet inscribed by my mother. I reached for it, but he pulled away.

"Do you know what this is, Jay?"

"My mother gave—"

"Your mother?" He laughed. "This— This is...or should I say *was*? This *was* the source of your power. Without this, Jay, you are Jake. You are *nothing!* When you were swapped—when you were changelinged—your mother gave you this amulet. It allows you to draw your elven power into the world of men. We elves cannot walk easily in this world. We inhabit what your father would call a parallel dimension. It is very close, and we share many things—the trees, the rivers, even animals. And we know how to step through. But staying there, using our powers, is not easy. Elves who live among men must use these." He held it up again and smiled. "Without your amulet, Jay, you are nothing."

"Give it back to me."

He leveled his sword at me again. He was grinning. He said, "On your knees. Time to die."

I shook my head. I wasn't feeling brave, but I felt a fury building inside me. "The thing with this world and any other world, Ar En, is that *none* of us gets out alive. So it's down to what my Viking ancestors used to say, isn't it? It isn't a question of whether you die. It's a question of how you die. And I plan to live and die on my feet. So if you're going to kill me, do it now. I won't kneel for you."

He raised an eyebrow. "So be it." He gripped the hilt with both hands and swung back the blade.

I stiffened my sinews and swore to myself I would not

135

wince. But before he struck, I said, "But as you kill me, Ar En, take a gift from me. The gift of knowledge. Know this, that you have looked so deep into your enemy's eyes that you have become your enemy. You rage against humans for having a black heart. But how much blacker does a heart get than when one brother kills another? Let me tell you this. You hate humanity because of its species, not because of what they do, because look at you. You are doing the very thing you claim you hate in them."

His face darkened, he curled his lip and swung back his blade. He stepped forward, let out a terrible roar and brought his sword crashing toward my neck. Then everything seemed to happen in slow motion. A great peace descended on me. I think I even smiled. I held his eye, unwavering, as I saw the keen silver blade slice through the air. I saw the look of madness in his eyes. I saw his hair fly across his face, and his teeth bared between snarling lips. Then the impossible happened. He seemed to shudder and falter. His eyes widened, staring past me. His jaw dropped and he opened his hands on the hilt of his sword. I saw him stumble back, his arms flailing as the blade tumbled to the ground, embedding itself in the turf.

I spun around to see what had caused his reaction.

She was easily thirty-feet tall. Her face was a mask of radiance. It was probably the most weirdly beautiful thing I had ever seen or could ever hope to see. It was like burnished silver, but at the same time, it was like you could see the whole cosmos through it — or in it. It was at once solid and transparent. Her eyes had no pupils. They were empty spaces that both saw everything and, if you had enough courage to look into them, therein you would see everything. But in her extreme beauty, she was also terrible and terrifying.

Her silver hair streamed out to an impossible length and seemed to entwine itself in the trees and the grass and the flowers and all living things, and errant strands seemed to lose themselves among the stars. Her robe also was silver, but as it moved in the breeze, a million different translucent, electric colors flashed and flowed across it—violet, chrome green, electric blue, acid yellow. And from her back, four vast dragonfly wings quivered and shimmered against the night sky. And when she spoke, her voice was both overpowering and quiet, gentle and terrifying.

"Would you spill the blood of an elf-son, Ar En?"

I turned. He had dropped to his knees, as he had wanted me to do. Tears were streaming down his face, but rage was in his eyes. He pointed a trembling finger at me. "But he betrays us! His destiny is with man!"

Her voice cut him dead. It seemed to come from the air itself, as though the light of the stars was speaking. "I look into your heart, Ar En, and I see only blackness. The world you wish to save does not spring from darkness but from light and love…"

Ar En struggled to his feet, his anger overcoming his terror. He indicated the woodlands and the hills under the moon. "Does man love the bear, the whale, the tiger? Does man love the living beings he exterminates day after day? Does man love the grass he will scorch from the face of his Mother Earth? Does man love the elf, the gnome or the fairy, whom he has driven to the brink of extinction? Does man love the naga, whom he has driven underground, into hiding? And now he will bring fire raining down on his mother and scorch her to the brink of very extinction!"

She remained impassive, with all of eternity gazing through her eyes. She said, "Would you be like man, then, Ar En?"

"No!" He stepped toward her, defiant now in his anger. "I would survive! And I would have the elven folk survive and our brethren the naga and the gnomes and all the children of the Earth Mother!" He gestured toward her. "You say I have blackness and hate in my heart, but does the fox hate the rabbit that it kills and eats? Does the hawk hate the dove? Does the lion hate the fawn? No! He must survive and he does what he must. And I say to you, Danu, that man must be *expunged* from our world and be cast back into the void before he destroys us!" And he pointed at me without looking at me, "And this…this *traitor* will fight to establish man's dominion on our Earth!"

My head was reeling. I wanted to tell him to stop. He had me confused with somebody else. But somewhere inside I knew that there was some kind of twisted truth in his words. I was shaking my head at him and saying, "No… no…*no!*" but he couldn't see or hear me — or *wouldn't* see or hear me.

The being he had called Danu spoke. "Hern does not hate his prey, Ar En. There is no hatred or cruelty in the heart of the true hunter. He lives in the cycle of life and death. When his time comes, he dies well. And while he lives, he lives with courage and a bountiful heart. But you, Ar En, have lost your way. You have strayed from your path. You may die with courage, but you do not live well. You live in the shadow of your hatred. Go from me and learn to love. When you have found love, come back."

She reached out her hand and a bead of light appeared on her fingertip. There was a huge flash and the last thing I saw was Ar En, in stark silhouette, spiraling into a vortex of intense light. I heard his wailing scream then there was silence. I bent and retrieved my mother's amulet.

* * * *

There was no moon. It happened quite suddenly. The sky was a peaceful, clear blue with a few early autumn clouds suspended motionless in the heavens. There was no fire. The crumbling walls of the abbey stood about us, silent and ancient. There was no Danu, no Ar En, not even Dicky.

I was sitting with my back against the wall and my rucksack by my side. The door through which we had stepped was on my right, closed. Ciara had her head on my shoulder and she was sleeping. Beyond her, Sebastian was curled up on the grass, also sleeping, as was Ciara's dad. I felt for my sword and my bow, but they weren't there. I felt for my cell. That wasn't there, either.

I gently touched Ciara's face. She opened her eyes and, as she focused on me, I knew that there was full knowledge in them. She smiled, reached out and touched my cheek and we kissed.

I said, "Do you remember?"

She didn't answer. She said, "What time is it?"

I checked my watch. "My God, it's half past three!"

She smiled again. "You have a debate to attend, Mr. Norgard."

I looked at her in astonishment. "You cannot be serious!"

Her face told me she was. "Deadly. You promised."

"But, after everything that happened last night—"

"Jake Norgard, if you ever want to see me again, you *will* keep your promise." She turned and shook Sebastian and called out to her father, "Daddy, wake up!"

They both stirred and sat a moment, peering around them. Finally, Fionn scowled. "What in the name of sweet Jesus…?"

Ciara got to her feet and stared down at him with her hands on her hips. "*Don't!* I have had just about enough of you and your miserable griping!" His eyes bulged and his jaw dropped, but she plowed right on. "Now, you listen to me, Mr. Michael Fionn! I am *not* your prisoner. I am your *daughter*. Are you able to see the difference? Can you *understand* the difference?"

He struggled to a sitting position and made to get up. "Ciara!"

She leaned forward. "Don't 'Ciara' me. You know what happened to us, Daddy? Do you *know* what happened to us?" He stammered. She interrupted him. "We were kidnapped and held *prisoner*." They stared at each other. Before he could speak, she launched at him again. "Did you enjoy it, Daddy? Was it fun? Did you feel *good* about it?"

"*Ciara!*"

"I said *don't* 'Ciara' me! It was *horrible*, wasn't it? Being a *prisoner*? Well, that has been my life for the past two years and I am *sick* of it!" She straightened up and tidied her hair and her blouse. "Now that we have that cleared up, I have some things I have to say to you. First, that young man" — she pointed at me and Michael Fionn glanced at me sidelong — "*that* young man rescued us and saved *both* our lives. Do you appreciate that?" She waited.

He muttered.

She repeated, "Do you appreciate that, Daddy?"

"*Yes!* For Jaysus sake!"

"*Good!* Because from now on he is my official *boyfriend*! And don't you dare say a word against him!"

I don't know who gaped the widest, Fionn or me. We stared at each other then at Ciara then at each other again, and I do believe that a secret bond was formed between us in that moment.

"Second, this afternoon at six, Jake has a debate at the school. You *will* come along and you will *listen*, attentively, to everything he has to say. Understood?"

He nodded dumbly, gaping at her. Sebastian, who had been watching this whole performance with an expression of mild wonder on his face, coughed politely. "Does anyone have any idea of where exactly we are?"

Fionn stared at him as though he had no idea what Sebastian was talking about, then blinked and said, "Yes! This is St Mary's Abbey. It's just outside Little Sodbury."

Ciara said, "How far outside?"

He shrugged. "I don't know. A couple of miles. Why?"

Sebastian said, "Because we need to get back to Oxford on the double if we are going to get to the debate on time."

"And how do you propose to do that?"

I smiled. "In your car."

He stared at me. It was his day for staring at people. He said, "What?"

Sebastian struggled to his feet. "It would seem, Mr. Fionn, that your daughter is not the only thing this young scallywag has half-inched from you."

Fionn got to his feet and so did I, preparing to apologize. I said, "Mr. Fionn, it was to rescue your daughter. I would never have dreamed—"

He faced me and raised his hand, shaking his head. "Don't even think of apologizing, young man...Jake. Ciara is right. I have been a damned fool, and it has taken this to make me realize it. You're a grand young man, and I applaud my daughter's judgment. Welcome to the Fionn clan. I am proud to call you my friend."

He solemnly held out his hand, and we shook. And I manfully fought down a small lump in my throat while Sebastian and Ciara looked on, smiling.

All good.

Chapter Seventeen

The Jag was where we had left it. I fished out the keys from my pocket and opened the driver's door, but when Ciara's dad coughed and scowled at me, I handed them over, grinned and climbed in the back with Ciara. There we sat, holding hands and smiling secretly at each other. I guess to anyone watching, it would have been nauseating, but we were in heaven.

Sebastian sat in the passenger seat and we took off at a goodly speed toward Oxford.

After a while, I said to Ciara, "Why is it so important to you that I do this debate, Ciara? I haven't prepared a thing. I'm going to be slaughtered. Besides, I very much doubt Dicky is going to show."

She just appeared obstinate and said, "Trust me. You have to do it."

I ignored her and went on. "And why is it so important that your dad hears the debate. All he's going to see is me going, 'Umm...errr...erm...' and turning scarlet like a tongue-tied beetroot."

Fionn glanced at me in the rearview and spoke up. "Let me guess. The debate is about the environment. Am I right?"

I said, "Pretty much. 'Man Has the Right and the Duty to Exploit the Planet's Fossil Fuel Resources.'"

"And you have to argue against that proposition. Right again?"

"Yes, sir. You are."

"Well, there's your answer. For the last two years I've been drawing up a report for the European Commission on whether Europe should sanction the exploitation of oil reserves under Greenland. I've come under *extreme* pressure from certain interested parties — in particular, the Nixon Corporation — to advise in favor. I have received threats to my life, which I disregarded. Then I received threats against Ciara, which I shall not have. I make no bones about it. As those interests have requested, I am taking a hard-headed economic approach, and in my report, I am going to advise the commission to go ahead and drill for oil." He was silent then said, "You've seen the lengths they'll go to achieve their ends. But Ciara is on me day and night not to do it. I suppose she hopes that with your eloquence and reasoning, you'll persuade me not to. Well, let me tell you, young man, you've your work cut out for you. I will not put my daughter at risk, especially not from these…*creatures!*"

"Oh, boy…" I flopped back in the seat. My heart sank. Not only was I going to make a compete fool of myself, but I was also going to let down my dad *and* Ciara. *No pressure, Jake.*

But as we sped through the country lanes, I kept getting flashes of the weird experience I'd had at the abbey while Ciara and the others had slept. I kept hearing Ar En's impassioned pleas, both to me and to Danu. And, as irony would have it, I was now racing to a confrontation with that very same man to argue his point while he defended the opposite. I glanced at Ciara. She was smiling a secret smile at me, like she knew something I did not.

Eventually we skidded to a halt outside the school at half past five. We all piled out of the car and ran along the drive to the main door. The headmaster was there, receiving people with a look of extreme consternation on his face. He had over two hundred people in his audience, including diplomats, politicians and captains of industry, and, up to that moment, he either had no debaters or just one, with nobody to debate against. He stared at me aghast. Then he stared aghast at Michael Fionn, then at all of us as a group, with collective aghastness. I followed his gaze, first at myself then at my companions. We were scratched, bruised and muddy. Our hair was matted and uncombed and our clothes were torn.

He said, "Mr. Norgard, would you care to explain?"

But Fionn cut him dead. In a huge, booming Irish brogue he roared, "Do not even dream of questioning the boy. He is a hero. And what he has done in the past twelve hours will earn him a medal. Let the boy do his thing, and lead me to my seat before I pass out."

They left me and were ushered into the debating hall. The headmaster looked me over and said, "There is no time to clean up. Take your seat in the speakers' corner, by the stage. And for goodness' sake, comb your hair or something."

He walked away and I hastily ran my fingers through my mop then squeezed along the front row of the hall, feeling the eyes of over two hundred people on me. Among them, I saw my dad and Rosie sitting near the back. Dad seemed worried and not a little annoyed. Rosie was just disturbingly beautiful and cheerful, as always.

Then, as I arrived at the speakers' corner, I stopped dead in my tracks. Brutus was sitting leering at me, and by his side was Dicky, appearing spruce, dashing and handsome with one leg crossed over the other, watching me approach.

He raised an eyebrow at me and said, "Good of you to join us, Norgard. Some kind of hold-up?"

"Nothing I couldn't handle."

He smiled. "Manage to prepare much?"

I sat and assessed him. He was unbelievable. I had to admit I had a grudging respect for the guy. "I have some ideas," I said. "I had some inspiration during the night. You might be surprised."

"I don't doubt it. You're a surprising chap."

I glanced at him, but there was no hint of irony in his voice or on his face. Without thinking, I said, "Yeah, well, it runs in the family."

He seemed not to hear.

Then, Mr. Singh stepped onto the stage. I felt a hot pellet

of anxiety sear through my belly. He cleared his throat and began to speak. The school had an ancient tradition of debating, and many of its alumni had cut their teeth here and gone on to be among the greatest orators in the English Parliament at Westminster and at the House of Representatives and the Senate. This year, the debating teams had once again excelled, and he looked forward to an illuminating, lively and challenging debate. He failed to point out that neither of the two young men there today had been part of those teams or that one of them had done absolutely no preparation and no debating to date. He did, however, ask the audience to put their hands together for Mr. Richard Nixon of the Hern team, "who will argue in favor of the controversial proposition that, 'Man Has the Right and the Duty to Exploit the Planet's Fossil Fuel Resources.'"

There was polite applause and Dicky sprang—he had to spring. Guys like him always 'spring'—lithely onto the stage and stepped to the lectern, as though he'd been doing it all his life since he'd popped out of his mother's womb. I could just see him, as they were snipping the umbilical cord, "Doctors, nurses, may I first of all thank you for my warm welcome into this world..."

I snapped out of my surreal fantasy and watched him. He was taking his time, looking carefully at each section of the audience. He delayed too long and that made them uncomfortable, nervous on his behalf, so when he did start to speak, they would be anxious to support him. When he finally opened his mouth, his voice was strong and confident, with just enough arrogance to carry the sheep but not enough to offend the wolves.

He said, "The planet is dying. Temperatures are rising, deserts are spreading, the ice caps are melting. The planet is getting hotter." He paused, nodded and smiled. "For anyone who has spent the winter in England, that can only be good news." They laughed for him, as he knew they would. His delivery and his timing were faultless. He went on, "But

I am only partly joking. In the last ten to fifteen thousand years, humanity's relationship with the planet has changed beyond all recognition. From being vulnerable, weak bipeds at the mercy of our environment, we have become masters of the planet, and it is the environment—the planet itself—that is at *our* mercy. Some, the bleeding hearts, the Greens and the sandaled, woolly-hatted lentil stirrers of the world, will tell you that this is a bad thing. I am here to tell you that they are wrong."

He paused, looking again from face to face, like a man who has all the time in the world—like a man who is in perfect control, like a man that you follow.

"It is *not!*" and his words echoed around the chamber. "It is *not* the destiny of man to sit in a yurt gazing up at the stars, eating brown rice and healing his wounds with lavender oil. It is *not* man's destiny to break his bag in a brutish cycle of struggle, year after year, with the unforgiving earth.

"It *is* man's destiny to build space ships to explore the stars, to reach with his mind and his hands to distant planets, to send men and women to Titan and Jupiter, to sail the methane oceans of Neptune, to explore Alpha Centauri and send robots to the heart of the sun. It *is* the destiny of humanity to conquer the solar system, to master the mysteries of faster-than-light space travel, to conquer disease, to overcome old age and live to five hundred or a thousand years, acquiring wisdom and understanding surpassing anything we know today."

He paused, his words ringing out around the chamber. The audience was bewitched. He smiled, gave a small laugh. "You can't do that from a yurt. To do all that, you need observatories, laboratories. You need hospitals, research facilities and foundations. You need plastic, rubber, steel. You need electricity, you need *machines* and you need more machines to build those machines... *That* is called *industry!* And let's be clear, ladies and gentlemen, you can't run that kind of industry on windmills.

"For that kind of industry, you need atomic energy, coal

and oil..."

He fastened his eyes on Fionn and he let the words hang there in the air, like a belch at the vicar's tea party. I was fascinated. My head — not for the first time that day — was reeling. Was this the same guy who had tried to decapitate me a few hours earlier because, according to him, I supported those who were destroying his precious Mother Earth? I was agog.

He plowed on with his irresistible style, explaining in minute detail how the cycles of the earth led it through periods of glaciation and periods of extreme heat. He pointed out that sixty-five million years ago, the planet had been up to ten degrees hotter than it was now and modern scientists were bleating about a mere two-degree increase. He pointed out that a warmer planet would be a more stable planet, and how a hundred more years of oil and coal could lead us to finally creating the fusion reactor that would give us universal nuclear energy.

"Think!" he said, as though thinking meant necessarily agreeing with him. "Think! If instead of castrating industry, we embrace and manage the changes it brings to our world. We can use that energy to develop the holy grail in energy sources — the fusion reactor. One fusion reactor, ladies and gentlemen, can provide the world with as much energy as the sun, and enable us as a species to fulfill our potential and our destiny.

"Let us not slide backward into a new age of superstition, ignorance and tedious inedible food because we are afraid of the consequences of our genius. Let us instead drive forward and blaze a trail to a better world, a better life and the universe at our feet!"

There was tremendous applause. People burst out laughing, stood, clapped wildly and cheered. It was more like a rock concert than an Oxford debate. I glanced over at Ciara. She was watching me with no expression. Next to her, her dad was on his feet, clapping vigorously. Dicky held up a hand. The room fell silent.

"Thank you so much. It is heart-warming to see so much good sense among such eminently useful people. Please do welcome now, my friend Jake Norgard, who will try to persuade you all to live in yurts."

He left the stage among a storm of applause and laughter. He had them in the palm of his hand. And I had…well, absolutely nothing to say. I walked to the lectern, smiling, as the applause changed from uproarious approval to polite welcome.

I stood, smiling, waiting for the applause to stop. When it had, I looked back at Dicky and gave a small laugh. "Thank you, Dicky." To the audience, I said, "He's a very funny young man. A comedian. Fortunately, he doesn't expect anyone to take him seriously." There was some laughter but not like the laughter he'd got. I examined their faces — Ciara's, full of love and hope, her dad's, full of curiosity and interest and Sebastian's full of concern. The rest, attentive, listening, hoping to hear something of value. I smiled.

"I don't live in a yurt. And I hope that none of you do. I live in a Tudor manor that has been fitted out with all the latest modern conveniences, and I wouldn't have it any other way, unless I was in an apartment overlooking San Francisco Bay. So please, be reassured, I do not believe that humanity's destiny is to live in yurts and eat brown rice and lentils. In fact, in many ways, I agree with my brother's vision of humanity's destiny.

"But I take into account something which he, apparently, wants to ignore. And that is that we are not alone."

I looked at him. He was staring at me fixedly. I turned back to the audience. They were interested and curious as to what I was going to say next. I was pretty curious myself. I glanced over at Ciara, and as I peered into her eyes across the room, I felt my heart open and I began again to speak.

I shook my head. "We are not alone. I do not only mean that we share this earth with whales and polar bears and rhinos — though we do. I mean that we share this earth with trillions of species, each of which is imbued with a spark of life and a spark of intelligence. We are not the only species in this world that has a destiny. Every living creature in this world — and infinite other worlds — has a destiny. And though we should embrace ours, fearlessly, and explore the moons of Jupiter and the oceans of Neptune, we should not do so as a self-seeking, predatory species bent on the destruction of all those who stand in our way. We should do so as compassionate creatures and bringers of light. And before we take our compassion and our light to Titan or Neptune, we should make use of it right here on Earth."

I paused and gazed again into their faces. Not an eyelid fluttered. And I realized, with some surprise, that they were, quite literally, spellbound. I don't recall exactly what happened next. I think I bewitched myself. I seemed to go into some kind of trance. I recall, bizarrely, processions of images moving across the hall, and everybody there watching those images. There were images of a scorched, smoldering planet, wastelands peppered with carcasses and skeletons — some animal, some human. Jeeps and Land Rovers belched black smoke and flames. Factories disgorged billowing acid-smoke and gas. The oceans, like wastelands, steamed and boiled under a crimson sun.

I watched their faces as they watched the images that flowed from my mind and my mouth. It was like a bizarre, shared consciousness, as though I had taken them all by the hand into a parallel world within my own mind. I showed them, as though I were playing a long movie for them, the true consequences of their passive neglect and negligence. I showed them their world, their home, if they continued to allow themselves to be led on the path to apocalypse, and their faces showed dread — and horror. And when I looked at Michael Fionn, I saw his face, damp with tears.

I paused and knew I held them in my hand. And I said those words that possessed the most powerful magic in the world. I said, "But there is hope, and hope is all we need. We have options. We have possibilities. We have *potential!*

"All we need is to make better choices. If we have chased

the easy option, the quick fix, the instant gratification, and it has led us to the brink of destruction, then let's make longer movies in our minds about the consequences of our actions — and our inaction. Let's make the choices that lead to a world where we can be free and happy and healthy, where grass is green, the oceans are rich with life and the air is clean. Let us make the choices that lead to a world where people are free. Let us make the choices that lead to a world where *all* life — all conscious life — is respected, can live in dignity and grow to fulfill its destiny.

"We are not alone. We certainly have not the right — far less the obligation and duty — to exploit the planet's fossil fuel resources. We share the custody of Earth with all living beings. Let us be the custodians who finally, after fifteen thousand years, bring, instead of cruelty, greed and exploitation, light and compassion to our Mother Earth, and those who share her with us."

There was a timeless moment. It may have been a second or it may have been ten minutes or more, of absolute silence. Then the room erupted. They had been hypnotized, as had I, by my own words. I had taken them inside my consciousness, and I felt that I had walked through the landscapes of their minds. It had been a freaky experience, but somehow, by some miracle, I had pulled it off.

I stepped down amid the applause and stood facing Dicky. The headmaster was on the stage speaking. I didn't listen. I said to Dicky, "What were you playing at? After everything that happened, after everything you said to Danu…"

He stared at me for a long moment then said, "You're a fool, Norgard. A bloody fool. You are naïve, and you have backed a loser. Get out of my way." And he pushed past me and out of the hall.

Then the assessment of the judges was being read out and I had won. In a kind of daze, I went up on the stage and received the award and the commendation, and there was lots of clapping and cheering. My dad was shaking my hand, Ciara and Rosie were kissing me on the cheek and Sebastian was slapping me on the back. Then we were pushing out toward the door, and my dad was talking to the headmaster and Mr. Singh, who was saying that he had known from the start I could do it.

I was alone with Michael Fionn, and he was shaking my hand and shaking his head at the same time. "I had never seen it in that way, my boy. You put in such a way, with such clarity. I go to Brussels tomorrow with a new vision, with renewed hope. Thank you, young man. You are a remarkable fellow. Thank you..."

I stood alone among the crowd of people. I was aware that Ciara was watching me. I was aware that something was very wrong and she knew it. Everything was back to front and upside down. I had won. I had gotten through to Fionn, which I now understood was what I had been meant to do from the start. Everything had gone according to plan.

But still, something was very wrong.

Chapter Eighteen

Dad was shaking my hand and pounding me on the shoulder. We were out on the street and the evening breeze was chilling my face. I was smiling a lot. This was very different to what I had envisaged just an hour before.

Dad was saying, "Son, I cannot tell you how *proud* I am of you. My God, I had no idea you had this skill. You are one dark horse, Jake, but *wow!*" He turned to Rosie, who had a beautiful smile on her face. It was an odd smile. It reminded me of something, but I just couldn't think what it was. Dad was saying to her, "I mean, that boy was good. He had us all laughing and almost believing that climate change was a good thing." He turned back to me. "But, man! You came in there and *pow!* Jake, I am *so* proud of you!"

Rosie took my hand in both of hers. "I am very proud of you, too, Jake. You shone. There is no other word for it."

Sebastian came up and slapped me on the shoulder. He appeared a wreck, but I guess I looked the same. He shook me by the hand and said, "Good stuff, old chap. Proud of you." He shook Dad's hand, too, and Rosie's.

Dad was feeling expansive and said, "Listen, guys. I'm in the mood for celebrating. Tomorrow's Saturday and we don't need to rise early. How about it? Dinner on me. We'll go to Don Giovani's. And, Sebastian, we'd love you to join us." He gave me a sly smile and added, "And while you're at it, you can tell us all about what the hell happened today!"

Sebastian was saying he'd love to, but he needed half an hour to go home, shower and change. Over Dad's shoulder, I could see Ciara and Fionn climbing into the Jag. A stab of adrenaline that felt like fear and apprehension set fire to my gut, and without knowing exactly why, I said, "Dad? Do you mind if I invite Ciara and her father?"

He seemed surprised and hesitated. Across the road, the doors of the Jag slammed. I said, "Dad?"

"Um, well, yes, of course! Have they left yet?"

I began to push past him. "They're just going. I'll catch them…" But as I said it, the engine roared into life and they pulled away. A voice in my head was shouting at me to run after them. To catch them. I knew I had to be with Ciara and her dad that night. It wasn't over. Somehow, it wasn't over yet.

I turned back to Dad. Rosie was watching me intently. Dad was frowning.

I said, "Listen. I'm a mess. Why don't you two walk on to the restaurant? I'll drive back, have a shower and call Ciara. I'll meet you at the restaurant in half an hour."

Dad was frowning harder. "I don't know, son."

Rosie said, "George?"

He looked at her. "Wha…?"

She smiled at him and patted his cheek. "I think Jake would like Ciara to come along. I think he might have some news for us later."

His eyes went wide and his mouth made a big 'O'. He nodded. "Okay, son, be quick."

Rosie smiled at me, but there was very little humor in her face. She said, "Be quick. There's a good boy."

Dad threw me the keys and I ran. I clambered into the Jeep and almost didn't bother with seat belts but didn't want to press my luck at this point. I burned rubber for minutes and screeched into Fionn's drive, skidding to a halt and kicking up gravel. I jumped out and ran to the door, ringing the bell and hammering on the wood with my fist.

Michael Fionn took too long to answer, considering the noise I was making. When he did finally open it, he kept it on the chain. He peered out at me through the crack, pale and drawn. This was not the same man who had been pumping my hand half an hour earlier. I said, "Mr. Fionn, I need to talk to you and Ciara."

His eyes swiveled right and left. "Ah, now, she's gone to bed. She's awful tired. I'm not long for bed myself. Excellent debate. Now, I must…" and he began to close the door.

Without thinking, I jammed my foot in the gap. I said, "Mr. Fionn, it's urgent. I think they may come back."

His face changed suddenly and he leaned forward between the door and the jamb. "For God's sake, lad, go! Get out of here. You've caused enough havoc. Go! Just go!"

I reached through and grabbed him by the scruff of the neck. I had that strength that only desperation can give you. I yanked hard, his face pushed through the gap and he gave a small, strangled shriek. I pressed my face close to his and hissed. "Don't you realize what he is going to do? Once he has made you do what he wants, he will first kill Ciara then he will kill you!"

He shook his head—or tried to in the confined space—and began to sob. "But if I don't do what he says, he'll kill her. I can't bear to lose her. I can't."

I growled, "Man up! Your only hope is to let me in. Let me in or I'll kick the door down and set fire to your house! *Do* it!"

His eyes bulged. "Okay." He fumbled with the chain and let me in.

I said, "Where are they?"

He pointed with a flapping hand. "My study."

I hesitated. A thought suddenly crystallized in my mind. I sprinted silently up the stairs and into Ciara's room. Her bow was leaning against the wall. I strung it and selected two arrows. That was all I needed. Then I ran back down the stairs and pushed into the study.

He was sitting behind the desk. He was smiling at me. He had known I would know, and he'd known I would come. In his hand, he held a revolver. It seemed like the sort of thing Dirty Harry might use and like it would do a lot of damage. He was turned sideways to me, facing Ciara.

Ciara was on a straight-backed chair. She was tied, hand and foot. She was in the middle of the room, slightly to my left, in front of the fireplace. Fionn was on the sofa, appearing gray. Dicky looked at my hands then up at my face. "You brought a bow. How sweet. But you know you can never defeat me — not in combat."

I nocked one of the arrows but didn't draw it. I said, "For all your talk at the abbey, you never intended to stop the drilling for oil, did you?"

He chuckled, focused on Ciara instead of me. "You're slow, Jake, but I'll give you this, you do eventually get there."

"You knew that Ciara was trying to persuade her father to advise against the drilling. How did you know that? I guess you used your shape-shifting leprechauns."

He glanced at me, a little surprised. "Leprechauns?" He laughed. "Don't be absurd. Leprechauns are cobblers. Those were simple demons."

"But the last thing you wanted was a change in policy on fossil fuels. You wanted them to keep right on changing the climate, didn't you?"

He gazed at me a while with no expression. Finally, he said, "Give it up, Jake. Tomorrow, Michael here will travel to the European Commission and he will advise them to go right ahead and drill for oil, and there is absolutely nothing you can do about it. Your little exercise in blarney was very impressive, but you haven't got what it takes. You are not ruthless enough. Try to stop me, and Ciara will die. It's that simple." He raised the gun for me to see. "I am as good a shot with one of these as I am with one of those." He indicated my bow, which I'd brought, thinking there might be trouble. "But this does a lot more damage."

Ciara spoke for the first time. "Why? Surely we all want the same thing? Surely we want to save Earth?"

I answered for him. "Earth, yes, but not humanity. He sees humanity as a plague, don't you, Ar En? You don't want them to reform. You want them to follow the course of all plagues and destroy themselves. You made the point at the debate. The planet has seen high temperatures and massive CO_2 levels before. The planet will recover. Some species thrive on those levels, don't they? Especially reptiles, like the naga. But not humanity. Humanity would become extinct by its own hand. And *that* was what you wanted all along."

He nodded, still smiling. "Bingo. And that is what I will get. I, Jake, and those who work with me. Do not think I am alone. We will, eventually, drive your disgusting species back where you came from."

I shook my head. "No."

He looked at me, faintly surprised. "No? Really? You need convincing?" He stood and directed the gun at Ciara's leg. "What shall it be? Her kneecap? Her shin?"

Fionn half-rose, his face crumpling, his hands outstretched. "No! No! Please! I'll do anything you say. Anything!"

Dicky frowned at him, one of those taunting, smiling frowns. "I don't know, Michael. I think Jake is getting to you. I think you both need to be convinced of my seriousness — of my commitment. I don't think you believe me capable…"

He pulled back the hammer. Ciara met his eye and her jaw was set firm. She said, "Daddy, whatever he does to me, you *know* the right thing to do."

And as she spoke the words, I drew and loosed. It took him completely by surprise. He didn't react. I knew he wouldn't, because the arrow was not directed at him. It was directed at the medallion I knew he had hanging around his neck. By the time the barb had torn through his shirt and ripped the pendant from his chest, I had the second arrow nocked. In slow motion, he turned and looked at me in astonishment, realizing too late what I had done. He glared and turned back toward Ciara. The gun wavered in his hand as he tightened his finger on the trigger, but by then, the second arrow had left the bow. It pierced his wrist at a hundred and fifty miles per hour. The impact made the hammer of the revolver smash down. The gun exploded and spat fire.

The bullet skimmed past Ciara's head and shattered the oak paneling on the wall. By then, I was already at the fireplace with the poker in my hand. Dicky was screaming, trying to rip the shaft from his wrist. He knew what was coming and needed something—anything—as a sword.

But it was too late. I lunged forward and plunged the poker into his heart. There was no blood, just an intense flash of white-blue light, a percussion and a terrible scream that faded like an echo.

I got a knife from the kitchen and cut Ciara free then poured her dad a very stiff glass of whiskey. Believe it or not, we actually joined my dad and Rosie for dinner at Don Giovani's, after I'd had a shower and combed my hair. We were a little late, but Dad was so pleased with me—and with the two Martinis he'd already had—that nobody seemed to mind. All in all, it was a good day.

Chapter Nineteen

The next day was Saturday, and in the afternoon, after a well-deserved rest, Ciara came to visit. At first, we were kind of shy. Up till then, we had only ever spoken to each other at school, in secret or while escaping from demons and kidnappers. We had a lot to learn about each other — what music we liked, what bands, what we wanted to do in the future...all that stuff.

As it turned out, we were pretty much on the same page about most things, and we seemed to do a lot of laughing. And I don't care if it's lame or corny or whatever, however much she laughed, I still heard silver bells and saw bluebirds flying. That's just the way she was.

At four, Rosie, being Rosie, made English tea. Drawn by the amazing smell, we had joined her in the kitchen, where she was baking a cake. We chatted with her for a bit then she said, "Why don't you two take the little garden table down to the arbor? I'll bring the tea out on a tray when it's ready."

I had a moment of apprehension, remembering what had happened the last two times I'd been down there, thinking about Ciara. But I put the thought to the back of my mind. I lifted the white wrought-iron table, and between us we carried three chairs. It took two trips, and when we'd set them up, I sat and she strolled about, smelling the roses while I watched her. Somewhere a blackbird was singing into the September afternoon. A bee was buzzing lazily among the flowers. The air was sweet and heavy.

Ciara said, "I love blackbirds. They have the most beautiful song of all. Don't you think?"

I nodded.

"Actually," she went on, "I love all birds, and all birds love me."

I laughed. "I remember."

We heard footsteps, and after a second, Rosie appeared with a tray, bearing salmon and cucumber sandwiches, a rich fruit cake and a pot of tea. She set it on the table, sat and began to pour. Then she handed me a cup and said, "Don't worry, Jake. Gorm won't be joining us."

I froze. "What?"

She smiled at me. Ciara came over from the roses and sat next to me. Rosie handed her a cup, saying, "You thought that the way to summon him was to come down here and think about Ciara."

Ciara looked at me, beamed and burst out laughing. "Jake! That's so sweet."

I stared, aghast, from one to the other. "You know? You both know?"

Rosie put her hand on mine. "I'm sorry, Jake. I had to use Gorm. It was the only way. He's an awful clod and he does forget everything. The poor love *is* three thousand years old. But it is *so* hard to get the help these days, even in Tír na nÓg."

I shook my head, gawping from Ciara to Rosie and back again. "But...but *why?*"

She put down the teapot and cut into the cake. "Well, imagine... If you'd known I knew, you'd have been constantly asking me questions. You'd have been all over the place, wouldn't you? As it was, you did a magnificent job of keeping it a secret from me and your father."

"So, who else...?"

"Nobody, just me and Ciara."

My head was still shaking like a toy Alsatian. "But, but, but...who *are* you?"

She stopped dead with a slice of cake halfway to a plate. Her face was suddenly radiant with love and a just a hint of sadness. She laid down the slice of cake and came and hunkered down in front of me, holding my hands in hers. "Jake, I know it's hard. You believe I am twenty-six, just a few years older than you and Ciara, but actually, I am five hundred years old, and I am your mother."

I went cold. The hair on my scalp prickled, but suddenly it all made sense. "Mom? My *real* mother?"

"Yes, Jake, it's me."

"But you can't stay here, in this world. You have to go back."

"Every so often, yes. I met your father and we fell in love. He is such a brilliant, kind, honorable man. He had no idea who or what I was, but we loved each other and I gave up Tír na nÓg to be with him, and we had you. But eventually I had to go back or die. Believe me, it broke my heart to leave you both. So much, in fact, that I had to return."

"That's why he fell for you so quickly…"

"He recognized me. He would never admit it – to me or to himself – but I know he did. And so did you."

I wiped my eyes and my cheeks and realized my face was wet. "Mom, how long before…?"

She laughed. "Oh, a good few years. Don't worry, but my powers will slowly wane. I don't mind. It is you who needs to fight on, not me. I am just happy to be with you and George again."

I frowned. "But what about Dicky? He's my brother? Is he your son?"

She shook her head, stood and went back to her seat. "No. He is of our clan, and so he has the same name. He is my sister's son. He is your cousin."

I turned to Ciara. "And you… You knew. Why didn't you tell me?"

She grinned as she bit into a huge slice of cake. "At first, I didn't realize. That's why I kept telling you it was impossible for us to be together. My mother gave me a prophecy – that I would meet, fall in love with and eventually marry a prince from Tír na nÓg. Well, who would ever have imagined he'd be an American?" She burst out laughing. *Silver bells. Bluebirds.* Then she turned to me again and smiled. "I wanted it to be you, but I didn't believe it. Then when I realized? Well, there was so much going on, and it was kind of fun keeping the secret." She gave me a funny look and added, "I'm surprised you didn't guess, what with the archery and the birds and everything."

Rosie said, "Ciara is Danu's daughter. The highest clan. We are of the En, also among the highest. I doubt you will ever go to Tír na nÓg, Jay, until the time comes to pass over and you leave this world. But back there, you are a powerful prince. Always remember that. And you're not here by any accident. You have a purpose. Humanity is coming of age, and it is time they learned to love the Mother, and we learn to live in peace with each other. If they don't, Ar En and his friends will triumph, and that will be a dreadful tragedy."

I sat, stunned, and thought about it. "So, the bow and the sword... That wasn't Gorm. That was you." She nodded. "And when we came out of the underground river..."

Ciara was shaking her head. "No, that was me. I knew that if we were going to deal with Ar En, it had to be in our world, where we could call on the help of my mother. And while we were there, you could get a glimpse of who you were and what it was all about. I used the tunnel to open a portal."

I thought more then turned to Rosie again. "But if you're my mother, I am not a changeling. I'm half-elf, half-human."

Rosie—Mom—laughed. "It was one of the *many* things Gorm got wrong. You aren't the changeling, Ciara is."

Ciara gazed and said, "I am the daughter of the moon, Danu. I was sent here to help you against Ar En. Ar means, The Bringer of Fire. Jay is the Bringer of Peace. You and I have a lot of work to do together, my prince..." and she grinned from ear to ear.

Above our heads, the September sun continued on its lazy way toward the west, and on the chimney pot, a black silhouette against the autumn sky, the blackbird sang out its long, complicated song into the gathering evening.

More books from Finch Books

Book one in The Abrasaxon's Daughter series

The dangerous quest to find her father and fix her shattered world brings Brianna more than she ever expected.

BATTALIONS OF OBLIVION

There can only be
one Dream Master

DREAM GUY

AZA CLARKE

Book one in the Battalions of Oblivion series

Every teen has dreams, but only Joe Knightley can make his dreams reality. Even the nightmares…

Book one in The Pathfinders series

As the end of the world begins, Carla and Tully hurtle through a wormhole five years forward in time, only to find they haven't missed the Apocalypse after all.

Book one in The Nightmare Crew series

Paul Wiseman, orphan and runaway, was looking for a family. He found one — and got a little more than he bargained for in the process.

About the Author

William Kingshart

William Kingshart was born in London but his parents, whom he describes as 'bohemians', moved to Ibiza when he was two. He grew up on the smallest of the Balearic Islands, bare-foot, wild and uncombed. He did not attend school, but for four years had a governess who disappeared one day when William was 12.

In his teens, he moved with his family to Cordoba on the Spanish mainland, where at 16 he got his first job, breaking in wild horses. At 19, still bare-foot, wild and uncombed, William moved to London, via Barcelona and Paris, to become a rock star. He is grateful to whatever gods watch over him for foiling that project. He retains a fond nostalgia for Led Zeppelin and the Eagles.

He flirted with academia in his 30s and became an Incorporated Linguist, a Barrister at the Inner Temple, a psychologist and a Master Practitioner of neuro-linguistic programming.

He has been married twice and has two beautiful daughters.

He thinks he might live in the south of Spain, but he isn't sure.

William Kingshart loves to hear from readers. You can find contact information, website details and an author profile page at https://www.finch-books.com/

www.ingramcontent.com/pod-product-compliance
Lightning Source LLC
Chambersburg PA
CBHW051827170626
46807CB00003B/1057